MW00647120

LEONE LEONI

LÉONE LÉON

31

George Sand

LEONE LEONI

Translated by George Burnham Ives

With a New Chronology of Her Life and Work

Academy Chicago Publishers

Chronology © Academy Chicago Publishers

Published in 1978 by
Academy Chicago Publishers
363 West Erie Street
Chicago, Illinois 60610

Reprinted in 1997

Printed and bound in the U.S.A.

No part of this book may be reproduced in any form
without the express written permission of the publisher.

Cover: Jean Antoine Watteau (1694–1721). Study for "La Famille."

Library of Congress Cataloging-in-Publication Data
Sand, George, pseud. of Mdm. Dudevant, 1804–1876.
    Leone Leoni.
    Reprint of the 1900 ed. published by G. Barrie, Philadelphia
    I. Title.
PZ3.S21Lef 1978   [PQ2407]   843'.8   77-28240
ISBN 0-915864-62-2
ISBN 0-915864-61-4 pbk.

GEORGE SAND: CHRONOLOGY

1804   July 1: Birth at 15 rue Meslée, Paris, to Maurice
Dupin and Sophie-Victoire Delaborde. Christened
Amantine-Lucile Aurore. Family moves to rue de
la Crande-Batelière, Paris.

1808   Aurore travels to Spain with her mother. They
join her father at the Palace de Godoy in Madrid
where he is serving in Napoleon's army under
General Murat. The family travels to Nohant in
France, the home of Maurice Dupin's mother,
born Marie-Aurore de Saxe, Comtesse de Horne,
daughter of the illegitimate son of King
Frederick-Augustus II of Poland.
Sept 16: Death of Maurice Dupin, age 30, in a fall
from a horse.

1809   Feb 3: Sophie-Victoire gives custody of Aurore to
Mme Dupin de Francueil, her mother-in-law, in
return for payment of Maurice's debts and a
pension of 1000 francs a year.

1810–1814   Winters in Paris at rue Neuve-des-Mathurins with
her grandmother. Visits from Sophie-Victoire.
Summers at Nohant.

1818–1820   Educated at the English Convent des Augustines
in Paris.

1820	Returns to Nohant. Studies with her father's tutor, Deschartres. Rides horseback in male clothing.
1821	Death of Mme Dupin de Francueil. Aurore inherits money, a house in Paris and the house at Nohant.
1822	Moves in with her mother at 80 rue St-Lazare, Paris. April: Meets Casimir-François Dudevant, son of Baron Dudevant, on a visit to the Duplessis family. September 10: Marries Dudevant. They move to Nohant in October.
1823	June 30: Maurice is born at Hôtel de Florence, 56 rue Neuve-des-Mathurins, Paris.
1824	Spring and summer at the Duplessis' at Plessis-Picard near Melun; autumn at a Parisian suburb, Ormesson; winter in an apartment at rue du Faubourg-St Honoré.
1825	Spring at Nohant. Aurore is ill in the summer. Dudevants travel to his family home in Gascony. Vacation in the Pyrenees where she meets Aurélian de Sèze and recovers her health. Nov 5: Writes long letter to Casimir confessing attraction to de Sèze. She gives him up. Winter in Gascony.
1827	Takes Stéphane de Grandsagne as lover. They meet in Paris.
1828	Sept 13: Birth of Solange.

1829   Writes *Voyage en Auvergne*, unpublished in her lifetime. Sees de Sèze.

1830   Visit to de Sèze in Bordeaux. Their correspondence ceases. She writes a novel, *Aimée*, which she later burns. Meets new lover, Jules Sandeau. Dec: Discovers Casimir's will, filled with antipathy toward her. Decides to separate from him, to spend half the year in Paris, leaving the children in Nohant.

1831   Jan 4: Moves to Paris, to 31 rue de Seine, to live secretly with Sandeau. Joins staff of *Le Figaro*. Writes three short stories: "La Molinara" (in *Figaro*), "La Prima Donna" (in *Revue de Paris*) and "La Fille d'Albano" (in *La Mode*).
April: Returns to Nohant for three months. Writes *Indiana*.
July: Moves to 25 Quai St-Michel, Paris.
Dec: Publishes *Rose et Blanche* in collaboration with Jules Sandeau. Book is signed Jules Sand.

1832   Travel between Paris and Nohant.
April: Brings Solange to Paris. Quarrels with Sandeau.
May: *Indiana* published.
Nov: Moves to 19 Quai Malaquais with Solange. *Valentine* published. Maurice sent by Casimir to the Lycée Henri Quatre in Paris.

1833   Breaks with Sandeau.
June: Meets Alfred de Musset.
Publishes *Lélia*.
Sept: To Fontainebleau with Musset.
Dec 10: To Italy with Musset.
Publishes novellas in various journals.

1834 Jan 19: Hotel Danieli in Venice. Musset attempts a break with Aurore, becomes ill. His physician is Pietro Pagello.
March 29: Musset returns to Paris. Aurore remains with Pagello. Publication of *André, Mattéa, Jacques, Léone Léoni* and the first *Lettres d'un Voyageur.*
July: Returns to Paris with Pagello.
Aug 24: Musset goes to Baden.
Aug 29: Aurore to Nohant.
Oct: Returns to Paris. Musset returns from Baden. Pagello returns to Venice.
Nov 25: Begins journal to de Musset.
Dec: Returns to Nohant.

1835 Jan: Returns to Paris.
Mar 6: Final break with de Musset.
Meets Michel de Bourges, her lawyer and political mentor.
Writes *Simon.*
Autumn: Returns to Nohant for Maurice's holiday.
Oct 19: Casimir threatens her physically. Begins suit for legal separation.
Dec 1: Judgment in her favor won by default.

1836 Feb 16: She wins second judgment. Casimir brings suit.
May 10, 11: Another verdict in her favor from civil court of La Chatre. Casimir appeals to a higher court.
July 25, 26: Trial in royal court of Bourges. Jury divided. Out-of-court settlement. Her fortune is divided with Casimir.
Aug: To Switzerland with Maurice and Solange, Franz Liszt and Aurore's friend Marie d'Agoult.
Autumn: Hôtel de la France, 15 rue Lafitte, Paris, with Liszt and d'Agoult. Meets Chopin.

1837   Jan: Returns to Nohant.
Publishes *Mauprat* in spring. Writes *Les Maîtres Mosaïstes*. Liszt and d'Agoult visit Nohant. Fatal illness of Sophie-Victoire in Paris. Visit to Fontainebleau. Writes *La Dernière Aldini*. Trip to Gascony to recover Solange, who has been kidnapped by Casimir.

1838   Writes *L'Orco* and *L'Uscoque*, two Venetian novels.
May: To Paris. Romance with Chopin.
Nov: Trip to Majorca with children and Chopin.
Writes *Spiridion*. *La Dernière Aldini* published.

1839   Feb: Leaves Majorca for three months in Marseilles. Then to Nohant.
Publishes *L'Uscoque, Spiridion* and revised *Lélia*.
Oct: Occupies adjoining apartments with Chopin until spring of 1841 at 16 rue Pigalle, Paris.
Summer is spent at Nohant, with Chopin as guest.

1840   Writes *Le Compagnon du Tour de France* and *Horace*. Influenced by Pierre Leroux. Publication of *Gabriel, Cosima*, a novel based on her play.

1841   Moves from rue Pigalle to 5 and 9 rue St-Lazare, Square d'Orléans, with Chopin. Publication of *Pauline.*

1842   Vols 1 and 2 of *Consuelo* published, and *Horace*. Chopin and Delacroix at Nohant. Publishes *Un Hiuer à Majorque.*

1843   Volumes 3–4 of *Consuelo* published, along with *Fanchette* and volumes 1–2 of *La Comtesse de Rudolstadt*, the sequel to *Consuelo*.

1844   *Jeanne* published, first of the pastoral novels. Also the last volumes of *La Comtesse de Rudolstadt*. Established liberal newspaper *L'Éclaireur*. Writes articles on *Politics and Socialism.*

1845 Publishes *Le Meunier d'Angibault.*

1846 Publishes *La Mare au Diable,* second pastoral novel, *Isidora* and *Teuerino.*

1847 Solange marries Auguste-Jean Clésinger. Estrangement from Chopin, who has sided with Solange in a family quarrel, and whose health is deteriorating. *Lucrezia Floriani, Le Péché de M. Antoine* and *Le Piccinino* published.

1848 On behalf of the Second Republic, writes government circulars, contributes to *Bulletins de la République* and publishes her newspaper *La Cause du Peuple.* Death of Solange's newborn daughter.

1849 *La Petite Fadette* published. Birth of Solange's daughter Jeanne-Gabriel. *François le Champi* successfully performed as a play at the Odéon theater in Parıs.

1850 Begins liason with Alexandre Manceau, Maurice's friend. *François le Champi* published as both play and novel.

1851 Republic falls. Plays *Claudie* and *Le Mariage de Victorine* published.

1852 Uses her influence with Louis Napoleon to save her friends from political reprisal. Solange and her husband quarrel, leave Jeanne-Gabriel with Sand at Nohant.

1853 Death of Michel de Bourges. *Les Maîtres Sonneurs, La Filleule, Mont-Reveche* published.

1854 Clésingers officially separated. Volumes 1–4 of *Histoire de ma Vie, Adriani* and *Flaminio* published.

1855 Jan 13: Death of Jeanne-Gabriel at school. Visit to Italy with Maurice and Alexandre Manceau. Vols 5–20 of *Histoire de Ma Vie* published.

1856 Does French adaptation of *As You Like It.*

1857 Death of Musset. Manceau buys cottage at Gargilesse for himself and Sand. *Le Diable aux Champs* and *La Daniella* published.

1858 Holidays at Gargilesse on River Creuse, 30 miles from Nohant, with Monceau. *Les Beaux Messieurs de Bois-Doré* published and *Légendes Rustiques,* illustrated by Maurice.

1859 Publishes *Elle et Lui, L'Homme de Neige, Les Dames Vertes, Promenades Autour d'un Village, La Guerre* and *Garibaldi.*

1860 Writes *La Ville Noire* and *Marquis de Villemer.* Nov: Contracts typhus or typhoid fever.

1862 Marriage of Maurice to Caroline Calametta. *Autour de la Table, Souvenirs et Impressions Litteraires* published.

1863 Marc-Antoine Dudevant born, son of Maurice and Caroline. Manceau and Maurice quarrel. *Mademoiselle La Quintinie* and *Pourquoi les Femmes à l'Academie?* published.

1864 Death of Marc-Antoine Dudevant. Play *Le Marquis de Villemer* presented. Moves from 3 rue Racine near the Odéon to 97 rue des Feuillantines. Leaves Nohant, because of difficulties with Maurice, to stay at Palaiseau with Manceau.

1865 Aug 21: Death of Manceau from tuberculosis, at Palaiseau. *La Confession d'une Jeune Fille* and *Laura* published.

1866 Birth of Aurore Dudevant to Maurice and Caroline. Visits Flaubert at Croisset, dedicates *Le Dernier Amour* to him. *Monsieur Sylvestre* published.

1867 Return to Nohant. Publishes *Le Dernier Amour*.

1868 Birth of Gabrielle Sand Dudevant.

1870 Play *L'Autre* with Sarah Bernhardt. *Pierre Qui Roule, Le Beau Laurence* and *Malgré Tout* published.

1871 Death of Casimir Dudevant. Seige of Paris. Sand protests Paris Commune. *Césarine Dietrich and Journal d'un Voyageur pendant la Guerre* published.

1872 Turgenev visits Nohant. *Francia* and *Nanon* published.

1873 Flaubert and Turgenev at Nohant. Travels in France. *Impressions et Souvenirs* and *Contes d'une Grand-mère* published.

1874 *Ma Soeur Jeanne* published.

1875 *Flamande* and *Les Deux Frères* published.

1876 June 8: Death of George Sand. *Le Tour de Percemont* and *Marianne Chevreuse* published.

INTRODUCTION

Being at Venice, in very cold weather and under very depressing circumstances, the carnival roaring and whistling outside with the icy north wind, I experienced the painful contrast which results from inward suffering, alone amid the wild excitement of a population of strangers.

I occupied a vast apartment in the former Nasi palace, now a hotel, which fronts on the quay, near the Bridge of Sighs. All travellers who have visited Venice know that hotel, but I doubt if many of them have ever happened to be there on Mardi Gras, in the heart of the classic carnival city, in a frame of mind so painfully meditative as mine.

Striving to escape the spleen by forcing my imagination to labor, I began at hazard a novel which opened with a description of the locality, of the festival out-of-doors and of the solemn apartment in which I was writing. The last book I had read before leaving Paris was *Manon Lescaut.* I had discussed it, or rather listened to others discussing it, and I had said to myself that to make Manon Lescaut a man and Desgrieux a woman would be worth trying, and would present many tragic opportunities, vice being often very near crime in man, and enthusiasm closely akin to despair in woman.

I wrote this book in a week and hardly read it over

(13)

before sending it to Paris. It had answered my purpose and expressed my thoughts ; I could have added nothing to it if I had thought it over. And why should a work of the imagination need to be thought over ? What moral could we expect to deduce from a fiction which everyone knows to be quite possible in the world of reality ? Some people who are very rigid in theory—no one knows just why—have pronounced it a dangerous book. After the lapse of twenty years, I look it over, and can detect no such tendency in it. The Leone Leoni type, although not untrue to life, is exceptional, thank God ! and I do not see that the infatuation he inspires in a weak mind is rewarded by very enviable joys. However, I have, at the present moment, a well-fixed opinion concerning the alleged *morals* of the novel, and I have expressed elsewhere my deliberate ideas thereon.

GEORGE SAND.

Nohant, January, 1853.

I

We were at Venice. The cold and the rain had driven the promenaders and the masks from the square and the quays. We could hear naught save the monotonous voice of the Adriatic in the distance, breaking on the islands, and from time to time the shouts of the watch aboard the frigate which guards the entrance to Canal Saint-George, and the answering hail from the custom-house schooner. It was a fine carnival evening inside the palaces and theatres, but outside, everything was dismal, and the street-lights were reflected in the streaming pavements, where the hurried footstep of a belated masker, wrapped in his cloak, echoed loudly from time to time.

We were alone in one of the rooms of the old Nasi palace, to-day transformed into a hotel, the best in Venice. A few candles scattered about the tables, and the blaze on the hearth only partially lighted the enormous room, and the flickering of the flame seemed to make the allegorical divinities painted in fresco on the ceiling move to and fro. Juliette was indisposed, and had refused to go out. Lying on a sofa and half-covered by a fur cloak, she seemed to be dozing; and I walked back and forth noiselessly on the thick carpet, smoking *Serraglio* cigarettes.

(15)

We recognize in my country a certain state of the mind which is, I think, peculiar to Spaniards. It is a sort of serious tranquillity which does not exclude activity of thought, as among the Teutonic races and in the cafés of the Orient. Our intellect does not grow dull during the trances in which we are buried. When we walk to and fro with measured step for hours at a time, on the same line of mosaics, without swerving a hair's breadth and puffing away at our cigars—that is the time when the operation that we may call mental digestion takes place most easily. Momentous resolutions are formed at such times, and excited passions calm down and give birth to vigorous acts. A Spaniard is never calmer than when he is meditating some scheme; it may be sinister or it may be sublime. As for myself, I was digesting my plan; but there was nothing heroic or alarming about it. When I had made the circuit of the room about sixty times and smoked a dozen cigarettes, my mind was made up. I halted by the sofa, and said to my young companion, regardless of her sleep:

"Juliette, will you be my wife?"

She opened her eyes and looked at me without answering. I thought that she had not heard me, and I repeated my question.

"I heard you very plainly," she replied in an indifferent tone—then held her peace anew.

I thought that my question had displeased her, and my anger and grief were terrible; but, from respect for Spanish gravity, I manifested neither, but began to pace the floor again.

At the seventh turn Juliette stopped me, saying: "What is the use?"

I made three turns more; then I threw away my cigarette, and, drawing a chair to her side, sat down.

"Your position in society must distress you?" I said
to her.

"I know," she replied, raising her exquisite face and
fixing upon mine her blue eyes wherein apathy seemed
to be always at odds with melancholy,—"yes, I know,
my dear Aleo, that I am branded in society with an inef-
faceable designation, that of kept mistress."

"We will efface it, Juliette; my name will purify
yours."

"Pride of the grandee!" she rejoined with a sigh.
Then, turning suddenly to me and seizing my hand,
which she put to her lips in spite of me, she added:
"Do you really mean that you will marry me, Bustamente? O my God! my God! what comparisons you
force me to make!"

"What do you mean, my dear child?" I asked her.
She did not reply, but burst into tears.

These tears, of which I understood the cause only too
well, hurt me terribly. But I concealed the species of
frenzy which they aroused in me and returned to my
seat by her side.

"Poor Juliette!" I said to her; "will that wound bleed
forever?"

"You gave me leave to weep," she replied; "that was
the first of our agreements."

"Weep, my poor afflicted darling," I said; "then
listen and answer me."

She wiped away her tears and put her hand in mine.

"Juliette," I said to her, "when you speak of yourself
as a kept woman, you are mad. Of what consequence
are the opinions and coarse remarks of a few fools? You
are my friend, my companion, my mistress."

"Alas! yes," she said, "I am your mistress, Aleo, and
it is that that dishonors me; I should have chosen to die

rather than to bequeath to a noble heart like yours the possession of a half extinct heart."

"We will rekindle the ashes gradually, my Juliette; let me hope that they still hide a spark which I can find."

"Yes, yes, I hope so, I wish that it may be so!" she said eagerly. "So I shall be your wife? But why? Shall I love you better for it? Will you feel surer of me?"

"I shall know that you are happier and I shall be happier for that reason."

"Happier! you are mistaken; I am as happy with you as possible; how can the title of Donna Bustamente make me any happier?"

"It would put you out of reach of the insolent disdain of society."

"Society!" said Juliette; "you mean your friends. What is society? I have never known. I have passed through life and made the tour of the globe, but have never been able to discover what you call society."

"I know that you have lived hitherto like the enchanted maiden in her globe of crystal, and yet I have seen you shed bitter tears over the deplorable position in which you then were. I made an inward vow to offer you my rank and my name as soon as I should be assured of your affection."

"You failed to understand me, Don Aleo, if you thought that shame made me weep. There was no place in my heart for shame; there were enough other causes of sorrow to fill it and make it insensible to everything that came from without. If he had continued to love me, I should have been happy, though I had been covered with infamy in the eyes of what you call society."

It was impossible for me to restrain a shudder of wrath;
I rose to pace the floor. Juliette detained me. "Forgive me," she said in a trembling voice, "forgive me for
the pain I cause you. It is beyond my strength always
to avoid speaking of him."

"Very well, Juliette," I said, stifling a painful sigh,
"pray speak of him if it is a relief to you! But is it possible that you cannot succeed in forgetting him, when
everything about you tends to direct your thoughts
toward another life, another happiness, another love?"

"Everything about me!" said Juliette excitedly; "are
we not in Venice?"

She rose and walked to the window; her white silk
petticoat fell in numberless folds about her graceful form.
Her chestnut hair escaped from the long pins of chased
gold which only half confined it, and bathed her back in
a flood of perfumed silk. She was so lovely with the
faint touch of color in her cheeks, and her half loving,
half bitter smile, that I forgot what she said and went to
her to take her in my arms. But she had drawn the
curtains partly aside, and looking through the glass, as
the moon's moist beams were beginning to break through
the clouds, she cried: "O Venice! how changed thou
art! how beautiful thou once wert in my eyes, and how
desolate and deserted thou dost seem to-day!"

"What do you say, Juliette?" I cried in my turn;
"have you been in Venice before? Why have you
never told me?"

"I saw that you wanted to see this beautiful city, and
I knew that a word would have prevented you from coming here. Why should I have made you change your
plan?"

"Yes, I would have changed it," I replied, stamping
my foot. "Even if we had been at the very gate of this

infernal city, I would have caused the boat to steer for some shore unstained by that memory; I would have taken you there, I would have swum with you in my arms, if I had had to choose between such a journey and this house, where perhaps you will find at every step a burning trace of his passage! But tell me, Juliette, where in heaven's name I can take refuge with you from the past? Mention some city, tell me of some corner of Italy to which that adventurer has not dragged you in his train?"

I was pale and trembling with wrath; Juliette turned slowly, gazed coldly at me, and said, turning her eyes once more to the window: "Venice, we loved thee in the old days, and to-day I cannot look on thee without emotion, for he was fond of thee, he constantly invoked thy name in his travels, he called thee his dear fatherland; for thou wert the cradle of his noble family, and one of thy palaces still bears the name that he bears."

"By death and eternity!" I said to Juliette, lowering my voice, "we leave this dear fatherland to-morrow!"

"*You* may leave Venice and Juliette to-morrow," she replied with frigid sang-froid; "but, as for me, I take orders from no one, and I shall leave Venice when I please."

"I believe that I understand you, mademoiselle," I said indignantly: "Leoni is in Venice."

Juliette started as if she had received an electric shock.

"What do you say? Leoni in Venice?" she cried, in a sort of frenzy, throwing herself in to my arms; "repeat what you said; repeat his name, let me at least hear his name once more!"

She burst into tears, and, suffocated by her sobs, almost lost consciousness. I carried her to the sofa, and without thinking of offering her any further assistance,

began to pace the edge of the carpet once more. But my
rage subsided as the sea subsides when the sirocco folds
its wings. A bitter grief succeeded my excitement; and
I fell to weeping like a woman.

II

In the midst of this heart-rending agitation, I paused a
few steps from Juliette and looked at her. Her face was
turned to the wall, but a mirror fifteen feet high, which
formed the panel, enabled me to see her face. She was
pale as death and her eyes were closed as in sleep; there
was more weariness than pain in the expression of her
face, and that expression accurately portrayed her mental plight: exhaustion and indifference triumphed over
the last ebullition of passion. I hoped.

I called her name softly and she looked at me with an
air of amazement, as if her memory lost the faculty of
retaining facts at the same time that her heart lost the
power to feel anger.

"What do you want," she said, "and why do you
wake me?"

"Juliette," I replied, "I offended you; forgive me;
I wounded your heart."

"No," she said, putting one hand to her forehead and
offering me the other, "you wounded my pride only. I
beg you, Aleo, remember that I have nothing, that I live
on your gifts, and that the thought of my dependent
state humiliates me. You are kind and generous to me,
I know. You lavish attentions on me, you cover me with

jewels, you overwhelm me with your luxury and your magnificence; but for you I should have died in some paupers' hospital, or should be confined in a madhouse. I know all that. But remember, Bustamente, that you have done it all in spite of me, that you took me in half-dead, and that you succored me when I had not the slightest desire to be succored ; remember that I wanted to die, and that you passed many nights at my pillow, holding my hands in yours to prevent me from killing myself ; remember that I refused for a long time your protection and your benefactions, and that, if I accept them to-day, it is half from weakness and discourage-ment, half from affection and gratitude to you, who ask me on your knees not to spurn them. Yours is the no-blest rôle, my friend, I know it well. But am I to blame because you are kind ? Can I be seriously reproached for debasing myself when, alone and desperate, I confide myself to the noblest heart on earth ? "

" My beloved," I said, pressing her to my heart, " you reply most convincingly to the vile insults of the miser-able wretches who have misrepresented you. But why do you say this to me ? Do you think that you need to justify yourself in the eyes of Bustamente for the hap-piness you have bestowed upon him—the only happiness he has ever enjoyed in his life ? It is for me to justify myself, if I can, for I am the one who has done wrong. I know how stubbornly your pride and your despair re-sisted me ; I am not likely ever to forget it. When I assume a tone of authority with you, I am a madman whom you must pardon, for my passion for you disturbs my reason and vanquishes all my strength of mind. Forgive me, Juliette, and forget a moment of anger. Alas ! I am unskilful in winning love. I have a natural roughness of manner which is unpleasant to you. I wound you when I am beginning to cure you, and I often destroy in one hour the work of many days."

"No, no, let us forget this quarrel," she interposed, kissing me. "For the little pain you cause me, I cause you a hundred times as much. You are sometimes imperious; my grief is always cruel. Do not believe, however, that it is incurable. Your kindness and your love will conquer it at last. I should have a most ungrateful heart if I did not accept the hope that you point out to me. We will talk of marriage another time; perhaps you will induce me to consent to it. However, I confess that I dread that species of servitude consecrated by all laws and all prejudices; it is honorable, but it is indissoluble."

"Still another cruel remark, Juliette! Are you afraid, pray, to belong to me forever?"

"No, no, of course not. Do not be distressed, I will do what you wish; but let us drop the subject for to-day."

"Very well, but grant me another favor in place of that; consent to leave Venice to-morrow."

"With all my heart. What do I care for Venice and all the rest? In heaven's name, don't believe me when I express regret for the past; it is irritation or madness that makes me speak so! The past! merciful heaven! Do you not know how many reasons I have for hating it? See how it has shattered me! How could I have the strength to grasp it again if it were given back to me?"

I kissed Juliette's hand to thank her for the effort she made in speaking thus, but I was not convinced; she had given me no satisfactory answer. I resumed my melancholy promenade about the room.

The sirocco had sprung up and dried the pavement in

an instant. The city had become resonant once more as it ordinarily is, and the thousand sounds of the festival reached our ears: the hoarse song of the tipsy gondoliers, the hooting of the masks coming from the cafés and guying the passers-by, the plash of oars in the canal. The guns of the frigate bade good-night to the echoes of the lagunes, which made answer like a discharge of artillery. The Austrian drum mingled its brutal roll, and the bell of St. Mark's gave forth a doleful sound.

A ghastly depression seized upon me. The candles, burning low, set fire to their green paper ruffles and cast a livid light upon the objects in the room. Everything assumed imaginary forms and made imaginary noises, to my disturbed senses. Juliette, lying on the sofa and swathed in fur and silk, seemed to me like a corpse wrapped in its shroud. The songs and laughter out of doors produced upon me the effect of shrieks of distress, and every gondola that glided under the marble bridge below my window suggested the idea of a drowning man struggling with the waves and death. Finally, I had none but thoughts of despair and death in my head, and I could not raise the weight which was crushing my breast.

At last, however, I succeeded in calming myself and reflected somewhat less wildly. I admitted to myself that Juliette's cure was progressing very slowly, and that, notwithstanding all the sacrifices in my favor which gratitude had wrung from her, her heart was almost as sick as at the very first. This long-continued and bitter regret for a love so unworthily bestowed seemed inexplicable to me, and I sought the cause in the powerlessness of my affection. It must be, I thought, that my character inspires an insurmountable repugnance which she

dares not avow to me. Perhaps the life I lead is unpleasant to her, and yet I have made my habits
conform to hers. Leoni used to take her constantly
from city to city. I have kept her travelling for two
years, forming no ties anywhere, and never delaying
for an instant to leave the place where I detected the
faintest sign of ennui on her face. And yet she is
melancholy, that is certain; nothing amuses her, and
it is only from consideration for me that she deigns sometimes to smile. Not one of the things that ordinarily give
pleasure to women has any influence on this sorrow
of hers; it is a rock that nothing can shake, a diamond
that nothing can dim. Poor Juliette! What strength
in your weakness! what desperate resistance in your
inertia!

I had unconsciously raised my voice until I expressed
my troubles aloud. Juliette had raised herself on one
arm and was listening to me sadly, leaning forward on
the cushions.

"Listen to me," I said, walking to her side, "I have
just imagined a new cause for your unhappiness. I have
repressed it too much, you have forced it back into your
heart too much, I have dreaded like a coward to see that
sore, the sight of which tears my heart; and you, through
generosity, have concealed it from me. Your wound,
thus neglected and abandoned, has become more inflamed
every day, whereas I should have dressed it and poured
balm upon it. I have done wrong, Juliette. You must
show me your sorrow, you must pour it out in my bosom,
you must talk to me about your past sufferings, tell me
of your life from moment to moment, name my enemy
to me. Yes, you must. Just now you said something
to me that I shall not forget; you implored me to let you
hear his name at least. Very well! let us pronounce it

together, that accursed name that burns your tongue and your heart. Let us talk of Leoni.''

Juliette's eyes shone with an involuntary gleam. I felt a terrible pang; but I conquered my suffering and asked her if she approved my plan.

"Yes," she said with a serious air, "I believe that you are right. You see, my breast is often filled with sobs; the fear of distressing you keeps me from giving them vent, and I pile up treasures of grief in my bosom. If I dared to display my feelings before you, I believe that I should suffer less. My sorrow is like a perfume that is kept always confined in a tightly closed box; open the box and it soon escapes. If I could talk constantly about Leoni and tell of the most trivial incidents of our love, I should bring under my eyes at the same moment all the good and all the harm he did me; whereas your aversion often seems to me unjust, and in the secret depths of my heart I make excuses for injuries which, if told by another, would be revolting to me.''

"Very well," said I, "I desire to learn them from your mouth. I have never known the details of this distressing story; I want you to tell them to me, to describe your whole life. When I am better acquainted with your troubles, perhaps I shall be better able to relieve them. Tell me all, Juliette; tell me by what means this Leoni succeeded in making you love him so dearly; tell me what charm, what secret he possessed; for I am weary of seeking in vain the impracticable road to your heart. Say on, I am listening.''

"Ah! yes, I am glad to do it; it will give me some relief at last. But let me talk and do not interrupt me by any sign of pain or anger; for I shall tell things as they happened; I shall tell the good and the bad, how I have loved and how I have suffered.''

"You must tell everything, and I will listen to everything," I replied.

I ordered fresh candles to be brought and rekindled the fire.

Juliette spoke thus:

III

You know that I am the daughter of a rich jeweller of Brussels. My father was skilful in his trade, but had little cultivation otherwise. He had raised himself from the position of a common workman to that of possessor of a handsome fortune which his flourishing business increased from day to day. Despite his lack of education, he was on terms of intimacy with the richest families in the province; and my mother, who was pretty and clever, was well received in the opulent society of the tradespeople.

My father was naturally mild and apathetic. Those qualities became more marked each day, as his wealth and comfort increased. My mother, being more active and younger, enjoyed unlimited freedom of action, and joyfully made the most of the advantages of wealth and the pleasures of society. She was kind-hearted, sincere and full of amiable qualities, but she was naturally frivolous, and her beauty, which was treated with marvellous respect by the years as they passed, prolonged her youth at the expense of my education. She loved me dearly, beyond question, but without prudence or discernment. Proud of my youthful charms and of the trivial talents

13

which she had caused me to acquire, she thought of
nothing but taking me about and exhibiting me; she took
a delicious but perilous pride in covering me constantly
with new jewels, and in appearing with me at parties. I
recall those days with pain and yet with pleasure; since
then, I have reflected sadly on the futile employment of
my early years, and yet I sigh for those days of careless
happiness which should never have ended or never have
begun. I fancy that I can still see my mother with her
plump, graceful figure, her white hands, her black eyes,
her coquettish smile, and withal so kind that you could
see at the first glance that she had never known anxiety
or vexation, and that she was incapable of imposing the
slightest restraint upon others, even with kindly intentions. Ah! yes, I remember her well! I remember our
long mornings devoted to planning and preparing our ball
dresses, our afternoons employed in making our toilets
with such painstaking care that hardly an hour remained
to show ourselves on the promenade. I see my mother,
with her satin dresses, her furs, her long white feathers,
and the whole fluffy mass of lace and ribbons. After finishing her toilet, she would forget herself a moment to
look after me. It was a great deal of a bore to unlace my
black satin boots in order to smooth out a wrinkle on the
instep or to try on twenty pairs of gloves before finding
one of a shade sufficiently delicate for her taste. Those
gloves fitted so tight that I often tore them after taking
the greatest pains about putting them on; then I must
begin anew, and we would have heaps of débris in front
of us before we had finally selected those that I was to
wear an hour, and then leave to my maid. However, I had
become so accustomed from childhood to regard these
trifling details as the 'most important occupations of a
woman's life, that I submitted patiently. We would set

out at last, and at the rustling of our silk gowns and the perfume exhaled by our handkerchiefs, people would turn to look after us. I was accustomed to hearing our names mentioned as we passed, by all sorts and conditions of men, and to see them glance curiously at my impassive face. This mixture of coldness and innocent effrontery constitutes what is called good breeding in a young woman. As for my mother, she felt a twofold pride in exhibiting herself and her daughter; I was a reflection, or, to speak more accurately, a part of herself, of her beauty, of her wealth; her good taste was displayed in my costume; my face, which resembled hers, reminded her as well as others of the scarcely impaired freshness of her early youth; so that, seeing my slender figure walking at her side, she fancied that she saw herself twice over, pale and delicate as she had been at fifteen, brilliant and beautiful as she still was. Not for anything in the world would she have gone out without me; she would have seemed to herself to be incomplete, half dressed as it were.

After dinner, the solemn discussion concerning ball dresses, silk stockings and flowers began anew. My father, who gave his whole attention to his shop during the day, would have preferred to pass the evening quietly by his fireside; but he was so easy-going, that he did not notice the way in which we deserted him. He would fall asleep in his chair while our hair-dressers were striving to understand my mother's scientifically devised plans. As we were going away, we would rouse the worthy man from his slumbers and he would go obligingly and take from his strong-box magnificent jewels mounted according to his own designs. He would fasten them himself about our arms and necks and take pleasure in remarking their effect. These jewels were intended for

sale. We often heard envious women about us crying
out at their splendor and whispering spiteful jests; but
my mother consoled herself by saying that the greatest
ladies wore what we had cast off, and that was true.
They would come to my father next day and order jewels
like those we had worn. A few days later he would
send the self-same ones; and we did not regret them, for
they were always replaced by others more beautiful.

Amid such surroundings, I grew up without thought for
the present or the future, without making any effort to
form or strengthen my character. I was naturally gentle
and trustful like my mother; I was content to float along
as she did on the current of destiny. I was less viva-
cious, however; I felt less keenly the attractions of pleasure and vanity; I seemed to lack the little strength that
she had, the desire and the faculty of constant diversion.
I accepted so easy a lot knowing nothing of its price, and
without comparing it with any other. I had no idea of
passion. I had been brought up as if I were never to
know it; my mother had been brought up in the same
way and considered that she was to be congratulated;
for she was incapable of feeling passion and had never
had any occasion to fight against it. My intelligence had
been applied to studies in which the heart had no occasion
to exercise control over itself. I performed brilliantly on
the piano, I danced beautifully, I painted in water-colors
with admirable precision and vigor; but there was
within me no spark of that sacred fire which gives life
and enables one to understand life. I loved my parents,
but I did not know what it was to love in any other way
than that. I was wonderfully clever in inditing a letter
to one of my young friends; but I had no more idea of
the value of words than of sentiments. I loved my girl
friends as a matter of habit, I was good to them because

I was obliging and gentle, but I did not trouble myself
about their characters; I scrutinized nothing. I made no
well-reasoned distinction between them; I was fondest
of the one who came oftenest to see me.

IV

I was the sort of person I have described, and sixteen
years old, when Leoni came to Brussels. The first time I
saw him was at the theatre. I was with my mother in a
box near the balcony, where he sat with several of the
richest and most fashionable young men in the city. My
mother called my attention to him. She was constantly
lying in wait for a husband for me, and always looked
for him among the men with the finest figures and the
most gorgeous clothes; those two points were everything
in her eyes. Birth and fortune attracted her only as accessories of things that she considered much more important—dress and manners. A man of superior mind in
a simple coat would have inspired nothing but contempt
in her. Her future son-in-law must have cuffs of a certain style, an irreproachable cravat, an exquisite figure,
a pretty face, coats made in Paris, and a stock of that
meaningless twaddle which makes a man fascinating in
society.

As for myself, I made no comparison between one man
and another. I blindly entrusted the selection to my
parents, and I neither dreaded nor shrank from marriage.

My mother considered Leoni fascinating. It is true
that his face is wonderfully beautiful, and that he has the

secret of being graceful, animated and perfectly at ease with his dandified clothes and manners. But I felt none of those romantic emotions which give to ardent hearts a foretaste of their destiny. I glanced at him for a moment in obedience to my mother, and should not have looked at him a second time, had she not forced me to do so by her constant exclamations and by her manifest curiosity to know his name. A young man of our acquaintance, whom she summoned in order to question him, informed her that he was a noble Venetian, a friend of one of the leading merchants of the city, that he seemed to have an enormous fortune, and that his name was Leone Leoni.

My mother was delighted with this information. The merchant who was Leoni's friend was to give a party the very next day, to which we were invited. Frivolous and credulous as she was, it was enough for her to have learned vaguely that Leoni was rich and noble, to induce her to cast her eyes upon him instantly. She spoke to me about him the same evening, and urged me to be pretty the next day. I smiled and went to sleep at precisely the same hour as on other nights, without the slightest acceleration of my heart beats at the thought of Leoni. I had become accustomed to listen without emotion to the formation of such projects. My mother declared that I was so sensible that they were not called upon to treat me like a child. The poor woman did not realize that she herself was much more of a child than I.

She dressed me with so much care and magnificence that I was proclaimed queen of the ball; but at first the time seemed to have been wasted: Leoni did not appear, and my mother thought that he had already left Brussels. Incapable of controlling her impatience, she asked the master of the house what had become of his Venetian.

"Ah!" said Monsieur Delpech, "you have noticed my

Venetian already, have you ? "—He glanced with a smile at my costume, and understood.—" He's an attractive youngster," he said, "of noble birth, and very much in fashion both in Paris and London; but it is my duty to inform you that he is a terrible gambler, and that the reason that you don't see him here is that he prefers the cards to the loveliest women."

"A gambler !" said my mother; "that's very bad."

"Oh! that depends," rejoined Monsieur Delpech. "When one has the means, you know!"

"To be sure!" said my mother; and that remark satisfied her. She worried no more about Leoni's passion for gambling.

A few seconds after this brief interview, Leoni appeared in the salon where we were dancing. I saw Monsieur Delpech whisper to him and glance at me, and Leoni's eyes wander uncertainly about me, until, guided by his friend's directions, he discovered me in the crowd and walked nearer to see me more distinctly. I realized at that moment that my rôle as a marriageable maiden was somewhat absurd; for there was a touch of irony in the admiration of his glance, and, for the first time in my life perhaps, I blushed and had a feeling of shame.

This shame became a sort of dull pain when I saw that Leoni had returned to the card room after a few moments. It seemed to me that I was laughed at and disdained, and I was vexed with my mother on that account. That had never happened before and she was amazed at the ill-humor I displayed toward her.—"Well, well," she said to me, with a little irritation on her side, "I don't know what the matter is with you, but you are turning homely. Let us go."

She had already risen when Leoni hurriedly crossed the room and invited her to waltz; that unhoped-for incident restored all her good-humor; she laughingly tossed me her fan and disappeared with him in the whirl.

As she was passionately fond of dancing, we were always accompanied to balls by an old aunt, my father's older sister, who acted as my chaperon when I was not invited to dance at the same time as my mother. Mademoiselle Agathe—that was what we called my aunt—was an old maid of a cold and even disposition. She had more common sense than the rest of the family, but she was not exempt from the tendency to vanity, which is the reef upon which all parvenus go to pieces. Although she cut a very melancholy figure at a ball, she never complained of the necessity of accompanying us; it was an opportunity for her to display in her old age some very beautiful gowns which she had never had the means to procure in her youth. She set great store by money therefore; but she was not equally accessible to all the seductions of society. She had a hatred of long standing for the nobles, and she never lost an opportunity to decry them and turn them to ridicule, which she did with much wit.

Shrewd and penetrating, accustomed to inaction and to keeping close watch on the actions of other people, she had understood the cause of my little fit of spleen. My mother's effusive chatter had apprised her of her views concerning Leoni, and the Venetian's face, amiable and proud and sneering, all at once, disclosed to her many things that my mother did not understand.

"Look, Juliette," she said, leaning toward me, "there's a great nobleman making sport of us."

I felt a painful thrill. What my aunt said corresponded with my forebodings. It was the first time that I had seen contempt for our bourgeoisie plainly written on a man's face. I had been brought up to laugh at the contempt

which the women hardly concealed from us, and to look
upon it as an indication of envy; but hitherto our beauty
had preserved us from the disdain of the men, and I
thought that Leoni was the most insolent creature that
ever lived. I had a horror of him, and when, after bringing my mother back to her seat, he invited me for the
following contradance, I haughtily declined. His face
expressed such amazement that I understood how confi-
dently he reckoned upon a warm reception. My pride
triumphed and I sat down beside my mother, declaring
that I was tired. Leoni left us, bowing low after the
Italian manner, and bestowing upon me a curious glance
in which there was a touch of his characteristic mockery.

My mother, amazed at my action, began to fear that I
might be capable of having a will of my own. She
talked to me gently, hoping that in a short time I would
consent to dance, and that Leoni would ask me again,
but I persisted in remaining in my seat. An hour or more
later we heard Leoni's name several times amid the confused murmuring of the ball; some one passing near us
said that he had lost six hundred louis.

"Very fine!" said my aunt dryly; "he will do well
to look out for some nice girl with a handsome dowry."

"Oh! he doesn't need to do that," somebody else replied, "he is so rich!"

"Look," said a third, "there he is dancing; he doesn't
look very anxious."

Leoni was dancing, in fact, and his features did not
display the slightest concern. He accosted us again,
paid my mother some insipid compliments with the facility
of a man in the best society, and then tried to make me
speak by putting questions to me indirectly. I maintained
an obstinate silence and he walked away with an indifferent air. My mother was in despair and took me home.

For the first time she scolded me and I sulked. My
aunt upheld me and declared that Leoni was an impertinent fellow and a scoundrel. My mother, who had never
been opposed to such a point, began to weep, and I did
the same.

By such petty agitations did the coming of Leoni, and
the unhappy destiny that he brought, begin to disturb
the profound peace in which I had always lived. I will
not tell you with so much detail what happened on the
following days. I do not remember so well, and the insatiable passion that I conceived for him always seems
to me like a strange dream which no effort of my reason
can reduce to order. This much is certain, that Leoni was
visibly piqued, surprised and disconcerted by my coldness, and that he began at once to treat me with a respect which satisfied my wounded pride. I saw him every
day at parties or out walking, and my aversion to him
speedily vanished before the extraordinary civilities and
humble attentions with which he overwhelmed me. In
vain did my aunt try to put me on my guard against the
arrogance of which she accused him. I was no longer
capable of feeling insulted by his manners or his words;
even his face had lost that suggestion of sarcasm which
had offended me at first. His glance acquired from day
to day an indescribable gentleness and affectionateness.
He seemed to think of nothing but me; he even sacrificed his taste for card-playing, and passed whole nights
dancing with my mother and me or talking with us. He
was soon invited to call at our house. I dreaded his call
a little. My aunt prophesied that he would find in our
home a thousand subjects of ridicule which he would
pretend not to notice but which would furnish him with
material for joking with his friends. He came, and, to
cap the climax, my father, who was standing at his shop-

door, brought him into the house that way. That house, which belonged to us, was very handsome, and my mother had had it decorated with exquisite taste ; but my father, who took no pleasure in anything outside of his business, was unwilling to transfer to any other building his cases of pearls and diamonds. That curtain of sparkling jewels behind the glass panels which guarded it was a magnificent spectacle, and my father said truly enough that there could be no more splendid decoration for a ground-floor. My mother, who had had hitherto only transitory flashes of ambition to be allied to the nobility, had never been humiliated to see her name carved in huge letters just below the balcony of her bedroom. But when, from that balcony, she saw Leoni cross the threshold of the fatal shop, she thought that we were lost and looked anxiously at me.

V

During the few days immediately preceding this, I had had the revelation of a hitherto unknown pride. I felt it awake within me now, and, impelled by an irresistible impulse, I determined to watch Leoni's manner as he talked with my father in his counting-room. He was slow about coming upstairs, and I rightly inferred that my father had detained him, to show him, as was his ingenuous custom, the marvels of his workmanship. I went resolutely down to the shop and entered, feigning surprise to find Leoni there. My mother had always forbidden me to enter the shop, her greatest fear being that I should be taken for a shopgirl. But I sometimes slipped away to go down and kiss my poor father, who had no greater joy than to receive me there. When I entered he uttered an exclamation of pleasure and said to Leoni : ' Look, look, monsieur le baron, what I have shown you amounts to nothing ; here is my loveliest diamond.' Leoni's face betrayed the keenest delight ; he smiled at my father with emotion and at me with passion. Never had such a glance met mine. I became red as fire. An unfamiliar feeling of joy and passion brought a tear to the brink of my eyelid as my father kissed me on the forehead.

We stood a few seconds without speaking ; then Leoni, taking up the conversation, found a way to say to my father everything that was most likely to flatter his self-esteem as an artist and tradesman. He seemed to take extreme pleasure in making him explain the process by which rough stones were transformed into precious gems, brilliant and transparent. He said some interesting things on that subject himself, and, addressing me, gave me some mineralogical information that was within my reach. I was confounded by the wit and grace with which he succeeded in exalting and ennobling our condition in our own eyes. He talked to us about products of the goldsmith's art which he had seen in his travels, and extolled especially the works of his compatriot Cellini, whom he placed beside Michael Angelo. In short, he ascribed so much merit to my father's profession and praised his talent so highly that I almost wondered whether I was the daughter of a hard-working mechanic or a genius.

My father accepted this last hypothesis, and, being charmed with the Venetian's manners, took him up to my mother. During this visit, Leoni displayed so much

wit and intelligence, and talked upon every subject in such
a superior way that I was fairly fascinated as I listened to
him. I had never conceived the idea of such a man.
Those who had been pointed out to me previously as the
most attractive were so insignificant and vapid beside
him that I thought I must be dreaming. I was too ignorant to appreciate all Leoni's knowledge and eloquence,
but I understood him instinctively. I was dominated by
his glance, enthralled by his tales, surprised and fascinated by every new resource that he developed.

It is certain that Leoni is a man endowed with extraordinary faculties. In a few days he succeeded in arousing
a general infatuation throughout the city. He has all the
talents, commands all the means of seduction. If he
were present at a concert, after a little urging he would
sing or play upon any instrument with a marked superiority over the professional musicians. If he consented to
pass the evening in the privacy of some family circle, he
would draw lovely pictures in the women's albums. In
an instant he would produce a portrait full of expression,
or a vigorous caricature; he improvised or declaimed in
all languages; he knew all the character dances of Europe, and he danced them all with fascinating grace; he
had seen, remembered, appreciated and understood
everything; he read the whole world like a book that one
carries in one's pocket. He acted admirably in tragedy
or comedy; he organized companies of amateurs; he was
himself leader of the orchestra, star performer, painter,
decorator and scene-shifter. He was at the head of all
the sports and all the parties. It could truly be said that
pleasure walked in his footprints, and that, at his approach, everything changed its aspect and assumed a
new face. He was listened to with enthusiasm and
blindly obeyed; people believed in him as a prophet;

and if he had promised to produce spring in midwinter, they would have deemed him capable of doing it. After he had been in Brussels a month, the character of the people had actually changed. Pleasure united all classes, soothed all the tender susceptibilities, brought all ranks to the same level. It was nothing but riding-parties, fireworks, theatricals, concerts and masquerades. Leoni was magnificent and generous; the workmen would have risen in revolt for him. He scattered favors about with lavish hand, and found money and time for everything. His caprices were soon adopted by everybody. All the women loved him, and the men were so subjugated by him that they did not think of being jealous of him.

How, amid such infatuation, could I remain insensible to the glory of being distinguished by the man who made fanatics of a whole province! Leoni overwhelmed us with attentions and surrounded us with respectful homage. My mother and I had become the leaders of society in the city. We walked by his side at all the entertainments; he assisted us to display the most insane splendor; he designed our dresses and invented our fancy costumes; for he understood everything and at need would have made our gowns and our turbans himself. By such means did he take possession of the affections of the whole family. My aunt was the most difficult conquest. She held out for a long while and distressed us by her discouraging remarks.—Leoni was a man of evil habits, she said, a frantic gambler, who won and lost the fortune of twenty families every evening; he would devour ours in a single night. But Leoni undertook to soften her, and succeeded by laying hold of her vanity, that lever which he worked so vigorously while seeming only to touch it lightly. Soon there were no obstacles left. My hand was promised him, with a dowry of half a million. My aunt suggested that we should have more certain information concerning the fortune and rank of this foreigner. Leoni smiled and promised to furnish his patents of nobility and his title deeds within three weeks. He treated the matter of the marriage contract very lightly, but it was drawn with the utmost liberality toward him and confidence in him. He seemed hardly to know what I was to bring him. Monsieur Delpech, and, upon the strength of his assurance, all Leoni's new friends, declared that he was four times richer than we were, and that his marriage to me was a love-match. I readily allowed myself to be persuaded. I had never been deceived, and I never thought of forgers and blacklegs except as in the rags of poverty and the livery of degradation.

A wave of painful emotion almost suffocated Juliette. She paused and looked at me with a dazed expression.

"Poor child!" I said, "God should have protected you."

"Oh!" she rejoined, contracting her ebon eyebrows, "I used two terrible words; may God forgive me! I have no hatred in my heart, and I do not accuse Leoni of being a villain; no, no, for I do not blush for having loved him. He is an unfortunate man whom we should pity. If you knew—— But I will tell you all."

"Go on with your story," I said to her; "Leoni is guilty enough; you have no intention of accusing him more than he deserves."

Juliette resumed her narrative.

It is a fact that he loved me, loved me for myself; the sequel proved that clearly enough. Do not shake your head, Bustamente. Leoni's is a powerful body, animated by a vast mind; all the virtues and all the vices, all the passions, holy and guilty alike, find a place in it at the same time. No one has ever chosen to judge him impartially; he was quite right in saying that I alone have known him and done him justice.

The language that he used to me was so novel to my ear that I was intoxicated by it. Perhaps my absolute ignorance up to that time of everything bordering on sentiment made that language seem more delicious and more extraordinary to me than it would have seemed to a more experienced girl. But I believe—and other women believed with me—that no man on earth ever felt and expressed love like Leoni. Superior to other men in evil and in good, he spoke another tongue, he had another expression, he had also another heart. I have heard an Italian woman say that a bouquet in Leoni's hand was more fragrant than in another man's, and it was so with everything. He gave lustre to the simplest things and rejuvenated the oldest. There was a prestige about him; I was neither able nor desirous to escape its influence. I began to love him with all my strength.

At this period I seemed to grow in my own eyes. Whether it was the work of God, of Leoni, or of love, a vigorous mind developed and took possession of my feeble body. Every day I felt a world of new thoughts come to life within me. A word from Leoni gave birth to more sentiments than all the frivolous talk I had heard all my life. He observed my progress and was elated and proud over it. He sought to hasten it and brought me books. My mother looked at the gilt covers, the vellum and the pictures. She hardly glanced at the titles of the works which were destined to play havoc with my head and my heart. They were beautiful and pure books, almost all stories of women written by women: *Valérie, Eugène de Rothelin, Mademoiselle de Clermont, Delphine.* These

touching and impassioned narratives, these glimpses of
what was to me an ideal world, elevated my mind, but
they devoured it.   I became romantic, the most deplorable character that a woman can have.

VI

Three months had sufficed to bring about this meta-
morphosis.   I was on the eve of marrying Leoni.   Of all
the documents he had promised to furnish, his certificate
of birth and his patents of nobility alone had come to
hand.   As for the proofs of his wealth, he had written
for them to another lawyer, and they had not arrived.
He manifested extreme irritation and regret at this delay,
which caused a further postponement of our wedding.
One morning he came to our house with an air of desperation.   He showed us an unstamped letter, which he
had just received, he said, by a special messenger.   This
letter informed him that his man of business was dead,
and that his successor, having found his papers in great
disorder, had a difficult task before him to arrange them,
that he asked a further delay of one or two weeks
before he could furnish *his lordship* with the documents
he required.   Leoni was frantic at this mischance; he
would die of impatience and disappointment, he said, before the end of that frightful fortnight.   He threw himself down in a chair and burst into tears.

No, do not smile, Don Aleo, they were not pretended
tears.   I gave him my hand to console him; I felt that it

14

was wet with tears, and, moved by a thrill of sympathy, I too began to sob.

My poor mother could not stand it. She ran, weeping, to seek my father in his shop.—"It is hateful tyranny," she said, bringing him to where we were. "See those two unhappy children! how can you refuse to make them happy, when you see what they suffer? Do you want to kill your daughter out of respect for an absurd formality? Won't those papers arrive just as surely and be just as satisfactory after they have been married a week? What are you afraid of? Do you take our dear Leoni for an impostor? Can't you see that your insisting on having evidence of his fortune is insulting to him and cruel to Juliette?"

My father, bewildered by these reproaches, and above all else by my tears, swore that he had never dreamed of being so exacting, and that he would do whatever I wished. He kissed me a thousand times and talked to me as people talk to a child of six when they yield to his whims, to be rid of his shrieks. My aunt appeared on the scene and talked less tenderly. She even reproved me in a way that hurt me.—"A virtuous, well-bred young woman," she said, "ought not to show so much impatience to belong to a man."—"It's easy to see," said my mother, altogether out of patience, "that you never had the chance to belong to one."—My father could not endure any lack of consideration for his sister. He leaned toward her view, and remarked that our despair was mere childishness, that a week would soon pass. I was mortally wounded by the suspicion that I was impatient, and I tried to restrain my tears; but Leoni's exerted a magical influence over me, and I could not do it. Thereupon he rose, with moist eyes and glowing cheeks, and with a smile overflowing with hope and affection, went

to my aunt, took her hands in one of his, my father's in
the other, and fell on his knees, beseeching them not to
stand in the way of his happiness any longer. His manner, his tone, his expression had an irresistible power;
moreover, it was the first time that my aunt had ever seen
a man at her feet. Every trace of resistance was overcome. The banns were published, all the preliminary
formalities were gone through; our marriage was appointed for the following week, regardless of the arrival
of the papers.

The following day was Mardi Gras. Monsieur Delpech was to give a magnificent party, and Leoni had
asked us to dress in Turkish costumes; he made a charming sketch in water-color, which our dress-makers copied
almost perfectly. Velvet, embroidered satin and cash-
mere were not spared. But the quantity and beauty of
our jewels were what assured us an indisputable triumph
over all the other costumes at the ball. Almost all the
contents of my father's shop were made use of; we had
nets and aigrettes of diamonds, bouquets beautifully
mounted in stones of all colors. My waist, and even my
shoes, were embroidered with rare pearls; a rope of
pearls, of extraordinary beauty, served me as a girdle
and fell to my knees. We had great pipes and daggers
studded with sapphires and diamonds. My whole costume was worth at least a million.

Leoni accompanied us, dressed in a superb Turkish
costume. He was so handsome and so majestic in that
garb that people stood on benches to see him pass. My
heart beat violently, I was filled to bursting with a pride
that was almost delirium. My own costume was, as you
can imagine, the last thing in my mind. Leoni's beauty,
his success, his superiority to all the others, the sort of
worship that was paid him—and it was all mine, all at

my feet! that was enough to intoxicate an older brain than mine. It was the last day of my splendor! By what a world of misery and degradation have I paid for those empty triumphs!

My aunt, dressed as a Jewess, accompanied us, carrying fans and boxes of perfume. Leoni, who was determined to win her friendship, had designed her costume so artistically that he had almost given a touch of poetry to her serious, wrinkled face. She, too, was intoxicated, poor Agathe! Alas! what does a woman's commonsense amount to?

We had been there two or three hours. My mother was dancing and my aunt gossiping with the superannuated females who compose what is called in France the tapestry of a ball-room. Leoni was seated by my side and talking to me in an undertone with a passion of which every word kindled a spark in my blood. Suddenly his voice died on his lips; he became pale as death, as if he had seen a ghost. I followed the direction of his terrified glance and saw, a few steps away, a person the sight of whom was distasteful to myself: it was a young man named Henryet, who had made me an offer of marriage the year before. Although he was rich and of an honorable family, my mother had not deemed him worthy of me, and had dismissed him on the pretext of my extreme youth. But, at the beginning of the following year, he had renewed his offer with much persistence, and it had been currently reported in the city that he was madly in love with me. I had not deigned to take any notice of him, and my mother, who considered him too simple and too ordinary, had put an end to his assiduities rather abruptly. He had manifested more grief than anger, and had started immediately for Paris. Since then my aunt and my young friends had reproached me somewhat for my indifference with respect to him. He was, they said, a most excellent young man, thoroughly educated, and of a noble character. These reproaches had disgusted me. His unexpected appearance in the midst of the happiness I was enjoying with Leoni was most unpleasant to me, and had the effect upon me of a new reproof. I turned my face away and pretended not to have seen him, but the strange glance he bestowed upon me did not escape me. Leoni hastily grasped my arm, and asked me to come and take an ice in the next room; he added that the heat was distressing to him and made him nervous. I believed him, and thought that Henryet's glance expressed nothing more than jealousy. We went into the gallery. There were few people there, and I walked back and forth for some time, leaning on Leoni's arm. He was agitated and preoccupied. I manifested some uneasiness thereat, and he answered that it was not worth talking about; that he simply did not feel perfectly well.

He was beginning to recover himself when I saw that Henryet had followed us. I could not help showing my annoyance.

"Upon my word that man follows us like remorse," I whispered to Leoni. "Is it really a man? I can almost believe that it is a soul in distress returned from the other world."

"What man?" said Leoni, with a start. "What's his name? where is he? what does he want of us? do you know him?"

I told him in a few words what had happened, and begged him not to seem to notice Henryet's absurd actions. But Leoni did not reply; and I felt his hand, which held mine, become cold as death. A convulsive

shudder passed through his body, and I thought that he
was going to faint; but it was all over in an instant.

"My nerves are horribly upset," he said. "I believe
that I shall have to go to bed; my head is on fire, and
this turban weighs a hundred pounds."

"O *mon Dieu!*" said I, "if you go now, this night
will seem interminable to me, and the party stupid beyond endurance. Go into some more retired room and
try taking off your turban for a few moments; we will
ask for a few drops of ether to quiet your nerves."

"Yes, you are right, my dear, good Juliette, my angel.
There's a boudoir at the end of the gallery, where we
probably shall be alone; a moment of rest will cure
me."

As he spoke, he led me hastily in the direction of the
boudoir; he seemed to fly rather than walk. I heard
steps coming after us. I turned and saw Henryet coming
nearer and nearer and looking as if he were pursuing us.
I thought that he had gone mad. The terror which
Leoni could not hide put the finishing touch to the confusion of my ideas. A superstitious fear took possession
of me; my blood congealed as in a nightmare; and it
was impossible for me to take another step. At that moment Henryet overtook us and laid a hand, which seemed
to me metallic, on Leoni's shoulder. Leoni stood still,
as if struck by lightning, and nodded his head affirma-
tively, as if he had divined a question or an injunction in
that terrifying silence. Thereupon Henryet walked
away, and I felt that I could move my feet once more.
I had the strength to follow Leoni into the boudoir,
where I fell on an ottoman, as pale and terror-stricken
as he.

VII

He remained some time thus ; then, suddenly collecting his strength, he threw himself at my feet.

"Juliette," he said, "I am lost unless you love me to frenzy."

"O heaven! what does that mean?" I cried wildly, throwing my arms around his neck.

"And you do not love me that way!" he continued, in an agony of despair. "I am lost, am I not?"

"I love you with all the strength of my heart!" I cried, weeping. "What must I do to save you?"

"Ah! you would never consent!" he replied, with a discouraged air. "I am the most miserable of men ; you are the only woman I have ever loved, Juliette, and when I am on the point of possessing you, my heart, my life, I lose you forever! I have no choice but to die."

"*Mon Dieu! mon Dieu!*" I cried; "can't you speak? can't you tell me what you expect of me?"

"No, I cannot speak," he replied; "a ghastly secret, a frightful mystery overhangs my whole life, and I can never disclose it to you. To love me, to go with me, to comfort me, you would need to be more than a woman, more than angel, perhaps!"

"To love you! to go with you!" I repeated. "Shall I not be your wife in a few days? You have but a word to say; however great my sorrow and that of my parents, I will follow you to the end of the world, if it is your will."

"Is that true, O my Juliette?" he cried in a transport

of joy; "you will go with me? you will leave everything for me? Very well; if you love me as much as that, I am saved! Let us go, let us go at once!"

"What! can you think of such a thing, Leoni? Are we married?" said I.

"We cannot marry," he replied shortly, in a firm voice.

I was stricken dumb.

"And if you will not love me, if you will not fly with me," he continued, "I have but one course to take; that is, to kill myself."

He said this in such a determined tone that I shuddered from head to foot.

"In heaven's name what is happening to us?" I said; "is this a dream? Who can prevent our marrying, when everything is decided, when you have my father's word?"

"A word from the man who is in love with you, and who is determined to prevent you from being mine."

"I hate him and despise him!" I cried. "Where is he? I propose to make him feel the shame of such cowardly persecution and such a detestable vengeance. But how can he injure you, Leoni? are you not so far above his attacks that with a word you can pulverize him? Are not your virtue and your strength as pure and unassailable as gold? O heaven! I understand; you are ruined! the papers you have been expecting bring only bad news. Henryet knows it and threatens to tell my parents. His conduct is infamous; but have no fear, my parents are kind, they adore me; I will throw myself at their feet, I will threaten to go into a convent; you can appeal to them again as you did yesterday and you will persuade them, you may be sure. Am I not rich enough for two? My father will not choose to condemn me to die of grief;

my mother will intercede for me. We three together shall be stronger than my aunt to argue with him. Come, don't be distressed, Leoni, this cannot part us, it is impossible. If my parents should prove to be as sordid as that, then I would fly with you.''

''Let us fly then at once,'' said Leoni with an air of profound gloom ; ''for they will be inflexible. There is something in addition to my ruin, something infernal, which I cannot tell you. Are you kind? Are you the woman I have dreamed of and thought I had found in you? Are you capable of heroism? Do you understand great things, boundless devotion? Tell me, Juliette, tell me, are you simply an amiable, pretty woman from whom I shall part with regret, or are you an angel whom God has sent to me to save me from despair? Do you feel that there is something noble in sacrificing yourself for one you love? Does not your heart swell at the thought of holding in your hands a man's life and destiny and in consecrating your whole being to him? Ah! if only we could change our rôles! if I were in your place! With what joy, with what bliss I would sacrifice to you all my affections, all my duties!''

''Enough, Leoni!'' I replied, ''you drive me wild with your words. Mercy, mercy for my poor mother, for my poor father, for my honor! You wish to ruin me——''

''Ah! you think of all those people!'' he cried, ''and not of me! You weigh the sorrow of your parents, and you do not deign to put mine in the balance! You do not love me!''

I hid my face in my hands, I appealed to God, I listened to Leoni's sobs; I thought that I was going mad.

''Very well! you will have it so,'' I said, ''and you have the power; speak, tell me what you wish, and I must obey you ; have you not my mind and my will at your disposal ? ''

"We have very few minutes to lose," replied Leoni. "We must be away from here in an hour, or your flight will have become impossible. There is a vulture's eye hovering over us ; but if you consent, we will find a way to outwit him. Do you consent ? do you consent ? "

He pressed me frantically in his arms. Cries of agony escaped from his breast. I answered yes without knowing what I was saying.

"Well, then, go back at once to the ball-room," he said, "and show no excitement. If anybody questions you, say that you have been a little indisposed; but don't let them take you home. Dance if you must. Above all things, if Henryet speaks to you, don't irritate him; remember that for another hour my fate is in his hands. An hour hence I will come back in a domino. I will have this bit of ribbon in my hood. You will recognize it, won't you ? You will go with me, and above all else, you will be calm, impassive. You must think of all this; do you feel that you are strong enough ? ''

I rose and pressed my hands against my throbbing heart. My throat was on fire, my cheeks were burning with fever. I was like a drunken man.

"Come, come," he said to me; with that he pushed me into the ball-room and disappeared. My mother was looking for me. I could detect her anxiety in the distance, and to avoid her questions I hurriedly accepted an invitation to dance.

I danced, and I have no idea how I kept from falling when the dance was at an end, I had made such a mighty effort to get through it. When I returned to my place my mother was already on the floor, waltzing. She had seen me dancing, so her mind was at rest, and she began to enjoy herself once more. My aunt, instead of questioning me about my absence, scolded me. I preferred that, for I was not called upon to answer and to lie. One of my friends asked me with a terrified air what the matter was with me and why I had such a distressed expression on my face. I answered that I had just had a violent fit of coughing.—"You must rest," she said, "and not dance any more."

But I had decided to avoid my mother's glance; I was afraid of her anxiety, her affection and my remorse. I spied her handkerchief, which she had left on the bench; I picked it up, put it to my face, and, covering my mouth with it, devoured it with convulsive kisses. My friend thought that I was coughing again, for I pretended to cough. I did not know how to pass that fatal hour, barely half of which had dragged away. My aunt noticed that I was very hoarse and said that she was going to urge my mother to go home. I was terrified by that threat and instantly accepted another invitation. When I was in the midst of the dancers, I noticed that I had accepted an invitation to waltz. Like almost all girls, I never waltzed; but, when I recognized in the man who already had his arm about me the sinister face of Henryet, terror prevented my refusing. He led me away and the rapid movement took away the last remnant of my reasoning power. I asked myself if all that was taking place about me were not a vision; if I were not lying in bed with the fever, rather than whirling about in a waltz, like a mad woman, with a man whom I held in horror. And then I remembered that Leoni would soon come for me. I looked at my mother, who seemed to fly through the circle of dancers, so light of foot and heart was she. I said to myself that it was impossible, that I could not leave my mother thus. I felt that Henryet was holding

me very tight in his arms and that his eyes were devouring my face, which was turned toward his. I came
very near shrieking and flying from him. But I remembered Leoni's words: "My fate is in his hands for
another hour." So I resigned myself. We stopped for
a moment. He spoke to me. I did not hear what he
said, but answered with a wild sort of smile. At that
moment I felt something brush against my bare arms and
shoulders. I had no need to turn for I recognized the almost imperceptible breathing of Leoni. I asked to be
taken back to my place. Another moment and Leoni, in
a black domino, offered me his hand. I went with him.
We glided through the crowd, we escaped, by some
miracle, the jealous surveillance of Henryet and of my
mother's eyes, for she was looking for me again. The
very audacity with which I left the ball-room in the
presence of five hundred witnesses, to fly with Leoni,
prevented my flight from being noticed. We passed
through the throng in the dressing-rooms. Some people
who were getting their cloaks recognized us and were
astonished to see me going down the stairs without my
mother, but they also were going away and so would not
report what they had seen in the ball-room.

When we reached the court-yard, Leoni, dragging me
behind him, rushed to a side gate not used by carriages.
We ran a short distance along a dark street; the door of
a post-chaise opened, Leoni lifted me in, wrapped me in
a huge fur cloak, pulled a travelling cap over my head,
and in the twinkling of an eye Monsieur Delpech's brilliantly lighted house, the street and the city disappeared
behind us.

We travelled twenty-four hours without once leaving
the carriage. At each relay-house, Leoni raised the window a little, put his arm outside, tossed the postilions four

times their pay, hurriedly withdrew his arm and closed the window. I scarcely thought of complaining of fatigue or hunger; my teeth were clenched, my nerves tense; I could neither shed a tear nor say a word. Leoni seemed more disturbed by the fear of being pursued than by my suffering and grief.

We halted near a château a short distance from the road. We rang at a garden gate. A servant opened the gate after we had waited a long while. It was two o'clock in the morning. When he finally appeared, grumbling, he put his lantern to Leoni's face; he had no sooner recognized him than he lost himself in apologies and led us to the house. It seemed deserted and ill-kept. Nevertheless I was shown to a fairly comfortable chamber. In a moment a fire was lighted, the bed prepared, and a woman came to undress me. I had fallen into a sort of idiocy. The heat of the fire revivified me somewhat, and I discovered that I was in a night-dress, with my hair unbound, alone with Leoni; but he paid no attention to me; he was busy packing in a box the magnificent costume, the pearls and diamonds in which we were both arrayed a moment before. The jewels that Leoni wore belonged for the most part to my father. My mother, determined that his costume should not be less gorgeous than ours, had taken them from the shop and lent them to him without saying anything about it. When I saw all that wealth packed into a box, I was mortally ashamed of the species of theft we had committed, and I thanked Leoni for thinking about returning them to my father. I don't know what answer he made; he told me that I had four hours to sleep and begged me to make the best of them, without anxiety or grief. He kissed my bare feet and left me. I had not the courage to go to bed; I slept in an arm-chair by the fire. At six

o'clock in the morning they came and woke me, brought
me some chocolate and men's clothes. I breakfasted and
dressed myself with resignation. Leoni came for me, and
before daybreak we left that mysterious house, of which
I have never known the name or the precise location or
the owner; and the same is true of many other houses,
some handsome and some wretched, which were thrown
open to us, in all countries and at all hours, at the bare
mention of Leoni's name.

As we rode on, Leoni recovered his usual serenity of
manner and spoke to me with all his former affection.
Enslaved and bound to him by a blind passion, I was an
instrument whose every chord he played upon at will.
If he was pensive I became melancholy; if he was cheerful, I forgot all my sorrows and all my remorse to smile
at his jests; if he was passionate, I forgot the weariness
of my brain and the exhaustion caused by weeping; I
recovered strength enough to love him and to tell him of
my love.

VIII

We arrived at Geneva, where we remained only long
enough to rest. We soon travelled into the interior of
Switzerland and there laid aside all fear of pursuit and
discovery. Ever since our departure, Leoni's only thought
had been to make his way with me to some peaceful
rural retreat, there to live on love and poetry in a never-
ending tête-à-tête. That delicious dream was realized.
We found in one of the valleys near Lago Maggiore one

of the most picturesque of chalets in a fascinating situation. At a very small expense we had it arranged con-
veniently inside, and we hired it at the beginning of
April. We passed there six months of intoxicating bliss,
for which I shall thank God all my life, although He has
made me pay very dear for them. We were absolutely
alone and cut off from all relations with the world. We
were served by a young couple, good-humored, sturdy
country people, who added to our contentment by the
spectacle of that which they enjoyed. The woman did
the housework and the cooking, the husband drove to
pasture a cow and two goats, which composed all our live
stock, milked and made the cheese. We rose early, and,
when the weather was fine, breakfasted a short distance
from the house, in a pretty orchard, where the trees,
abandoned to the hand of nature, put forth dense
branches in every direction, less rich in fruit than in
flowers and foliage. Then we went out to drive in the
valley or climbed some mountain. We gradually adopted
the habit of taking long excursions, and every day discovered some new spot. Mountainous countries have
the peculiar charm that one can explore them for a long
time before one becomes acquainted with all their beauties and all their secrets. When we went on our longest
excursions, Joanne, our light-hearted major-domo, attended us with a basket of provisions, and nothing could
be more delightful than our lunches on the grass. Leoni
was easily satisfied except as to what he called the refec-
tory. At last, when we had found a little verdure-clad
shelf half-way down the slope of some deep gorge, shel-
tered from wind and sun, with a lovely view, and a brook
close at hand sweetened by aromatic plants, he would
himself arrange the repast on a white napkin spread on
the ground. He would send Joanne to pick strawberries

and plunge the wine into the cool water of the stream. He would light a spirit lamp and cook fresh eggs. By the same process I used to make excellent coffee after the cold meat and fruit. In this way we had something of the enjoyments of civilization amid the romantic beauties of the desert.

When the weather was bad, as was often the case in the early spring, we lighted a huge fire to keep the dampness from our little dwelling of fir; we surrounded ourselves with screens which Leoni sawed out, put together and painted with his own hand. We drank tea; and while he smoked a long Turkish pipe I read to him. We called those our Flemish days; while they were less exciting than the others, they were perhaps even pleasanter. Leoni had an admirable talent for apportioning the time so as to make life easy and agreeable. In the morning he would exert his mind to lay out a scheme for the day and arrange our occupations for the different hours; and when it was done he would come and submit it to me. I always found it admirable, and we always adhered strictly to it. In this way, ennui, which always pursues recluses and even lovers in their tête-à-têtes, never came near us. Leoni knew all that must be avoided and all that must be looked after to maintain mental tranquillity and bodily well-being. He would give me directions in his adroitly affectionate way; and, being as submissive to him as a slave to his master, I never opposed a single one of his wishes. He said, for instance, that the exchange of thoughts between two people who love each other is the sweetest thing imaginable, but that it may become the greatest curse if it is abused. So he regulated the hours of our interviews and the places where they were to be held. We worked all day; I looked after the housekeeping; I prepared dainty

dishes for him or folded his linen with my own hands.
He was extremely sensible of such petty refinements of
luxury, and found them doubly precious in our little her-
mitage. He, on his side, provided for all our needs and
remedied all the inconveniences of our isolation. He
had a little knowledge of all sorts of trades; he did
cabinet work, he put on locks, he made partitions with
wooden frames and painted paper panels, he prevented
chimneys from smoking, he grafted fruit trees, he di-
verted the course of a stream, so that we had a supply of
cool water near the house. He was always busy about
something useful, and he always did it well. When
these more important duties were performed, he painted
in water-colors, composed lovely landscapes from the
sketches we had made in our albums during our walks.
Sometimes he wandered about the valley alone, making
verses, and hurried home to repeat them to me. He
often found me in the stable with my apron full of aromatic herbs of which the goats were very fond. My two
lovely pets ate from my lap. One was pure white, without a speck; her name was *Snow;* she had a gentle,
melancholy air. The other was yellow like a chamois,
with black beard and legs. She was very young, with
a wild, saucy face; we called her *Doe.* The cow's
name was *Daisy.* She was red, with black stripes running transversely, like a tiger. She would put her head
on my shoulder; and when Leoni found me so, he called
me his Virgin at the Manger. He would toss me his
album and dictate his verses, which were almost always
addressed to me. They were hymns of love and happiness which seemed sublime to me, and which must have
been sublime. I would weep silently as I wrote them
down; and when I had finished, "Well," Leoni would
say, "do you think they are pretty bad?" At that I

15

would raise my tear-stained face to his ; he would laugh
and kiss me with the keenest delight.

Then he would sit down on the sweet-smelling hay and
read me poems in other languages, which he translated
with incredible rapidity and accuracy. Meanwhile I was
spinning in the half-light of the stable. One must be
familiar with the exquisite cleanliness of Swiss stables to
understand our choosing ours for our salon. It was trav-
ersed by a swift mountain stream which washed it clean
every moment, and which rejoiced our ears with its
gentle plashing. Tame pigeons drank at our feet, and
under the little arch through which the stream entered,
saucy sparrows hopped in to bathe and steal a few wisps
of hay. It was the coolest spot in warm days, when all
the windows were open, and the warmest on cold days,
when the smallest cracks were stuffed with straw and
furze. Leoni, when tired of reading, would often fall
asleep on the freshly-cut grass, and I would leave my
work to gaze at that beautiful face, which the serenity
of sleep made even nobler than before.

During these busy days we talked little, although
almost always together ; we would exchange an occa-
sional loving word or caress and encourage each other
in our work. But when the evening came, Leoni became
indolent in body and mentally active. Those were the
hours when he was most lovable, and he reserved them
for the outpouring of our affection. Fatigued, but not
unpleasantly, by his day's work, he would lie on the
moss at my feet, in a lonely spot near the house, on the
slope of the mountain. From there we would behold
the gorgeous sunset, the melancholy fading away of the
daylight, the grave and solemn coming of the night. We
knew the moment when all the stars would rise, and over
which peak each of them would begin to shine. Leoni

was thoroughly familiar with astronomy, but Joanne, too, knew that science of the shepherds after his manner, and he gave the stars other names, often more poetic and more expressive than ours. When Leoni had amused himself sufficiently with his rustic pedantry, he would send him away to play the *Ranz des Vaches* on his reed-pipe at the foot of the mountain. The shrill notes sounded indescribably sweet in the distance. Leoni would fall into a reverie which resembled a trance; and then, when it was quite dark, when the silence of the valley was no longer broken by aught save the plaintive cry of some cliff-dwelling bird, when the fireflies lighted their lamps in the grass about us and a soft breeze sighed through the firs over our heads, Leoni would seem to wake suddenly from a dream, as if to another life. His heart would take fire, his passionate eloquence would overflow my heart. He would talk to the skies, the wind, the echoes, to all nature with enthusiastic fervor; he would take me in his arms and overwhelm me with delirious caresses; then he would weep with love on my bosom, and, growing calmer, would talk to me in the sweetest, most intoxicating words.

Oh! how could I have failed to love that unequalled man, in his good and in his evil days? How lovable he was then! how beautiful! how becoming the sunburn was to his manly face, and with what profound respect it avoided the broad white forehead over the jet-black eyebrows! How well he knew how to love and to tell his love! What a genius he had for arranging life and making it beautiful! How could I have failed to have blind confidence in him? How could I have failed to accustom myself to absolute submission to him? All that he did, all that he said, was good and wise and noble. He was generous, sensitive, refined, heroic; he took pleasure in relieving the destitution or the infirmities of the poor who knocked at our door. One day he jumped into a stream, at the risk of his life, to save a young shepherd; one night he wandered through the snow-drifts, surrounded by the most awful dangers, to assist some travellers who had lost their way and whose cries of distress we had heard. Oh! how, how could I have distrusted Leoni? how could I have conceived any dread of the future? Do not tell me again that I am credulous and weak; the most strong-minded of women would have been subjugated forever by those six months of love. As for myself, I was absolutely enslaved; and my cruel remorse for having abandoned my parents, the thought of their grief, grew fainter day by day, and, finally, vanished almost entirely. Oh! how great was that man's power!

Juliette paused and fell into a melancholy reverie. A clock in the distance struck twelve. I suggested that she should rest. "No," said she, "if you are not tired of listening to me, I prefer to go on. I feel that I have undertaken a task that will be very painful for my poor heart, and that when I have finished I shall neither feel nor remember anything for several days. I prefer to make the most of the strength I have to-day."

"Yes, you are right, Juliette," I said. "Tear the steel from your breast, and you will be better afterward. But tell me, my poor child, how it was that Henryet's strange conduct at the ball and Leoni's craven submission at a glance from him did not leave a suspicion, a fear in your mind?"

"What could I fear?" replied Juliette. "I knew so little of the affairs of life and the baseness of society that I utterly failed to understand that mystery. Leoni had told me that there was a terible secret. I imagined

a thousand romantic catastrophes. It was the fashion
then in books to introduce characters burdened by the
most extraordinary and improbable maledictions. Plays
and novels alike teemed with sons of headsmen, heroic
spies, virtuous murderers and felons. One day I read
Frederick Styndall, another day, Cooper's *Spy* fell into
my hands. Remember that I was a mere child, and that
my mind was far behind my heart in my passion. I
fancied that society, being unjust and stupid, had placed
Leoni under its ban for some sublime imprudence, some
involuntary offence, or as the result of some savage
prejudice. I will even admit that my poor girlish brain
found an additional attraction in that impenetrable mystery, and that my woman's heart took fire at the opportunity of adventuring its entire destiny to repair a noble
and poetic misfortune."

"Leoni probably detected that romantic tendency and
played upon it?" I said.

"Yes," she replied, "he did. But if he took so much
trouble to deceive me, it was because he loved me, because he was determined to have my love at any price."

We were silent for a moment; then Juliette resumed
her narrative.

IX

The winter came at last; we had made our plans to
endure all its rigors rather than abandon our dear retreat.
Leoni told me that he had never been so happy, that I
was the only woman he had ever loved, that he was
ready to renounce the world in order to live and die in

my arms. His taste for dissipation, his passion for gambling—all had vanished, forgotten forever. Oh! how
grateful I was to see that man, who shone so in society
and was so flattered and courted, renounce without regret all the intoxicating joys of a life of excitement and
festivities, to shut himself up with me in a cottage! And
be sure, Don Aleo, that Leoni was not deceiving me at
that time. While it is true that he had very strong reasons for keeping out of sight, it is none the less certain
that he was happy in his retreat, and that he loved me
there. Could he have feigned that perfect serenity during six whole months, unchanged for a single day? And
why should he not have loved me? I was young and
fair, I had left everything for him and I adored him. Understand, I am no longer under any delusion as to his
character; I know everything and I will tell you the
whole truth. His character is very ugly and very beautiful; very vile and very grand; when one has not the
strength to hate the man, one must needs love him and
become his victim.

But the winter began so fiercely that our residence in
the valley became extremely dangerous. In a few days
the snow reached the level of our chalet; it threatened
to bury it and to cause our deaths by starvation. Leoni
insisted on remaining; he wanted to lay in a stock of
provisions and defy the enemy; but Joanne assured him
that we should inevitably be lost if we did not beat a retreat at once; that such a winter had not been seen for
ten years, and that when the thaw came the chalet would
be swept away like a feather by the avalanches, unless
Saint Bernard and Our Lady of the Snow-drifts should
save it by a miracle.

"If I were alone," said Leoni, "I would wait for a
miracle and laugh at the snow-drifts; but I have no

courage when you share my dangers. We will go away
to-morrow."

"We must do it," I said; "but where shall we go? I
shall be recognized and betrayed very soon; I shall be
compelled by force to return to my parents."

"There are a thousand ways of eluding men and laws,"
replied Leoni with a smile; "we can surely find one;
don't be alarmed; the whole world is at our disposal."

"And where shall we begin?" I asked, forcing myself
to smile too.

"I don't know yet," he replied, "but what does it
matter? we shall be together; where can we be unhappy?"

"Alas!" said I, "shall we ever be so happy as we
have been here?"

"Do you want to stay here?"

"No," I replied, "we should be happy no longer; in
presence of danger, we should always be alarmed for
each other."

We made preparations for our departure. Joanne passed
the day clearing the path by which we were to go.
During the night I had a strange experience, upon which
I have feared, many times since then, to meditate.

In the midst of a sound sleep I suddenly felt very cold
and woke up. I felt for Leoni at my side, but he was not
there; his place was cold, and the bedroom door was
ajar, admitting a current of ice-cold air. I waited a few
moments, but, as Leoni did not return, I began to be
alarmed, so I rose and hastily dressed myself. Even
then I waited before making up my mind to go out, re-
luctant to allow myself to be governed by any mere
childish anxiety. But he did not appear; an invincible
terror seized upon me, and I went out, scantily clad, with
the thermometer fifteen degrees below freezing. I was

afraid that Leoni might have gone to assist some poor
creatures who were lost in the snow, as had happened a
few nights before, and I was determined to follow and
find him. I called Joanne and his wife; they were sleeping so soundly that they did not hear me. Thereupon,
almost frantic with dread, I went to the edge of the little
palisaded platform which surrounded the chalet and saw
a faint light twinkling on the snow some distance away.
I fancied that I recognized the lantern that Leoni carried
on his relief expeditions. I ran toward it as rapidly as
the snow would allow me, sinking in up to my knees. I
tried to call him, but the cold made my teeth chatter, and
the wind, which blew in my face, intercepted my voice.
At last I came near to the light and could see Leoni distinctly; he was standing on the spot where I had first
seen him, holding a spade. I approached still nearer, the
snow deadening the sound of my footsteps, and finally
stood almost beside him, unseen by him. The light was
enclosed in its metal cylinder and shone through a slit on
the opposite side from me, directly upon him.

I saw then that he had shovelled away the snow and
dug into the earth; he was up to his knees in a hole he
had made.

This strange occupation, at such an hour and in such
severe weather, gave me an absurd fright. Leoni seemed
to be in extraordinary haste. From time to time he
glanced uneasily about; I crouched behind a rock for I
was terrified by the expression of his face. It seemed to
me that he would kill me if he should find me there. All
the fanciful, foolish stories I had read, all the strange
conjectures I had made concerning his secret, recurred to
my mind; I believed that he had come there to dig up a
corpse, and I almost fainted. I was somewhat reassured
when I saw him, after digging a little longer, take a box

from the hole. He scrutinized it closely, looked to see if the lock had been forced, then placed it on the edge of the hole and began to throw back the earth and snow, taking little pains to conceal the traces of his operation.

When I saw that he was ready to return to the house with his box, I was terribly afraid that he would discover my imprudent curiosity, and I fled as swiftly as I could. I made haste to throw my wet clothes into a corner and go back to bed, resolved to pretend to be fast asleep when he returned; but I had plenty of time to recover from my emotion, for it was more than half an hour before he reappeared.

I lost myself in conjectures concerning that mysterious box, which must have been buried on the mountain since our arrival, and was destined to accompany us, either as a talisman of safety or as an instrument of death. It seemed to me unlikely that it contained money; for it was of considerable size and yet Leoni had lifted it with one hand and without apparent effort. Perhaps it contained papers upon which his very existence depended. What impressed me most strongly was the idea that I had seen the box before; but it was impossible for me to remember when or where. This time its shape and color were engraved on my memory as if by a sort of fatal necessity. I had it before my eyes all night, and in my dreams I saw a multitude of strange objects come out of it: sometimes cards cut into curious shapes, sometimes bloody weapons; sometimes flowers, feathers and jewels; and sometimes bones, snakes, bits of gold, iron chains and anklets.

I was very careful not to question Leoni or to let him suspect my discovery. He had often said to me that on the day that I discovered his secret all would be at an end between us; and although he thanked me on his knees for believing blindly in him, he often gave me to understand that the slightest curiosity on my part would be distasteful to him. We started the next morning on mules, and travelled by post from the nearest town all the way to Venice.

There we alighted at one of those mysterious houses which Leoni seemed to have at his disposal in all countries. This one was dark, dilapidated and hidden away, as it were, in a deserted quarter of the city. He told me that it belonged to a friend of his who was absent; he begged me to try to put up with it for a day or two, adding that there were important reasons why he could not show himself in the city at once, but that, in twenty-four hours at the latest, I should be provided with suitable lodgings and should have no reason to complain of life in his native place.

We had just breakfasted in a cold, damp room, when a shabbily dressed man, with a disagreeable face and a sickly complexion, made his appearance, observing that Leoni had sent for him.

"Yes, yes, my dear Thaddeus," Leoni replied, hastily leaving the table; "I am glad to see you; let us go into another room and not bore madame with business matters."

An hour later Leoni came and kissed me; he seemed excited, but satisfied, as if he had won a victory.

"I must leave you for a few hours," he said; "I am going to have your new home made ready; we shall sleep there to-morrow night."

X

He was away all day. The next day he went out
early. He seemed very busy; but he was in a more
cheerful mood than I had yet seen him. That gave me
courage to endure the tedium of another twelve hours
and dispelled the melancholy impression that that cold
and silent house produced upon me. In the afternoon I
tried to distract my thoughts by going over it; it was
very old; some remnants of antiquated furniture, tattered hangings, and several pictures half consumed by
rats attracted my attention ; but an object even more interesting to me turned my thoughts in another direction.

As I entered the room where Leoni had slept, I saw the
famous box on the floor ; it was open and entirely empty.
An enormous weight was lifted from my mind. The unknown dragon confined in that box had taken flight! the
terrible destiny which it had seemed to me to forebode
no longer weighed upon us!—"Well, well," I said to myself with a smile, "Pandora's box is empty; hope has
remained behind for me."

As I was about to leave the room, I placed my foot on
a small bit of cotton wool which had been left lying on
the floor with some crumpled tissue paper. I felt something hard and stooped mechanically to pick it up.
My fingers felt the same hard substance through the cotton, and on pulling it apart I found a pin made of several
large diamonds, which I at once recognized as belonging
to my father, and which I had worn on the evening of
the last ball, to fasten a scarf on my shoulder. This in-

cident made such an impression on me that I thought no more of the box or of Leoni's secret. I was conscious of nothing but a vague feeling of uneasiness concerning the jewels I had carried with me in my flight, and to which I had not since given even a thought, supposing that Leoni had sent them back at once. The possibility that that had not been done was horrible to me ; and as soon as Leoni returned I asked him ingenuously :

" My dear, you didn't forget to send back my father's diamonds after we left Brussels, did you ? "

Leoni looked at me with a strange expression. He seemed to be trying to read in the lowest depths of my soul.

" Why don't you answer ? " I said ; " what is there so surprising in my question ? "

" What the devil does it mean ? " he replied calmly.

" It means that I went into your room to-day, and found this on your floor. Thereupon I feared that, in the excitement of our flight and the confusion of our travels, you might have forgotten to send back the other jewels. For my own part, I hardly reminded you of it ; my brain was in such a whirl."

As I concluded, I handed him the pin. I spoke so naturally and was so far from dreaming of suspecting him, that he saw it at once ; and, taking the pin with the utmost calmness, he said :

"*Parbleu!* I don't know what this means. Where did you find it ? Are you sure that it belonged to your father and was not left behind here by the people who occupied the house before us ? "

" Oh! yes," said I, " here is an almost imperceptible mark near the fastening ; it's my father's private mark. With a magnifying-glass you can see his cipher."

" Very good," he replied ; " then the pin must have

been left in one of our trunks, and I suppose I dropped it this morning when shaking some of my clothes. Luckily it's the only piece of jewelry we brought away by accident; all the rest was placed in charge of a reliable man and addressed to Delpech, who must have turned it over to your family. I don't believe that it is worth while to return this; it would excite your mother's grief anew for very little money."

"It is worth at least ten thousand francs," I said.

"Very well, keep it until you have an opportunity to send it back. By the way, are you ready? are the trunks locked? There is a gondola at the door and your house is waiting impatiently for you; supper is already served."

Half an hour later we stopped at the door of a magnificent palace. The stairways were covered with amaranth-colored carpets; the white marble rails with flowering orange-trees, in midwinter, and with light statues which seemed to lean over to salute us. The concierge and four servants came forward to assist us to disembark. Leoni took a candlestick from one of them and raised it so that I could read on the cornice of the peristyle, in silver letters on an azure ground: *Palazzo Leoni.*

"O my love," I cried, "you did not deceive us? You are rich and of noble birth and I am in your house!"

I went all over the palace with childlike delight. It was one of the finest in all Venice. The furniture and the hangings, fairly glistening with newness, had been copied from antique models, so that the paintings on the ceilings and the old-fashioned architecture harmonized perfectly with the new accessories. The luxury that we bourgeois and people of the North affect is so paltry, so vulgar, so slovenly, that I had never dreamed of such elegance. I walked through the vast galleries as through

an enchanted palace; all the objects about me were
of strange shapes, of unfamiliar aspect; I wondered if I
were dreaming, or if I were really the mistress and queen
of all those marvellous things. Moreover, that feudal
magnificence was a fresh source of enchantment to me.
I had never realized the pleasure or the advantage of
being noble. In France people no longer know what it
is, in Belgium they have never known. Here in Italy
the few remaining nobles are still proud and fond of display; the palaces are not demolished, but are allowed to
crumble away. Between those walls laden with trophies
and escutcheons, beneath those ceilings on which the
armorial bearings of the family were painted, face to
face with Leoni's ancestors painted by Titian and Veronese, some grave and stern in their long cloaks, others
elegant and gracious in their black satin doublets, I
understood that pride of rank which may be so attractive
and so becoming when it does not adorn a fool. All this
illustrious environment was so suited to Leoni that it
would be impossible for me, even to-day, to think of him
as a plebeian. He was the fitting descendant of those
men with black beards and alabaster hands, of the type
that Van Dyck has immortalized. He had their eagle-
like profile, their delicate and refined features, their tall
stature, their eyes, at once mocking and kindly. If those
portraits could have walked they would have walked as
he did; if they had spoken, they would have had his
voice.

"Can it be," I said, throwing my arms about him,
"that it was you, my lord, Signor Leone Leoni, who
were in that chalet among the goats and hens the other
day, with a pickaxe over your shoulder and a blouse on
your back? Was it you that lived that life for six months,
with a nameless, witless girl, who has no other merit

than her love for you? And you mean to keep me with you, you will love me always, and tell me so every morning, as at the chalet? Oh, it is a too exalted and too happy lot for me; I had not aspired so high, and it terrifies me at the same time that it intoxicates me."

"Do not be frightened," he said, with a smile, "be my companion and my queen forever. Now, come to supper; I have two guests to present to you. Arrange your hair and make yourself pretty; and when I call you my wife, don't open your eyes as if you were surprised."

We found an exquisite supper served on a table sparkling with porcelain, glass and plate. The two guests were presented to me with due solemnity; they were Venetians both, with attractive faces and refined manners, and, although very inferior to Leoni, they resembled him somewhat in their pronunciation and in the quality of their minds. I asked him in an undertone if they were kinsmen of his.

"Yes," he replied aloud, with a laugh, "they are my cousins."

"Of course," added one of them, who was addressed as the marquis, "we are all cousins."

The next day, instead of two guests, there were four or five different ones at each meal. In less than a week our house was inundated with intimate friends. These assiduous guests consumed many sweet hours that I might have passed alone with Leoni, but had to share with them all. But Leoni, after his long exile, seemed overjoyed to see his friends once more and to lead a gayer life. I could form no wish opposed to his, and I was happy to see him enjoying himself. To be sure, the society of those men was delightful. They were all young and refined, jovial or intelligent, amiable or entertaining. They had excellent manners, and most of them were men

of talent. Every morning we had music ; in the afternoon we went on the water ; after dinner we went to the
theatre ; and, on returning home, had supper and cards.
I did not enjoy looking on at this last amusement, in
which enormous sums changed hands every night. Leoni
had given me permission to retire after supper, and I
never failed. Little by little the number of our acquaintances increased so that I was bored and fatigued by them ;
but I said nothing about it. Leoni still seemed enchanted
by this dissipated life. All the dandies of all nations who
were then in Venice met by appointment at our house to
drink and gamble and sing. The best singers from the
theatres came often to mingle their voices with our in-
struments and with Leoni's voice, which was neither less
beautiful nor less skilfully managed than theirs. Despite
the fascination of this society, I felt more and more the
longing for repose. To be sure, we still had some pleasant hours tête-à-tête from time to time. The dandies did
not come every day, but the regular habitués consisted
of a dozen or more men who formed the nucleus of our
dinner-parties. Leoni was so fond of them that I could
not help feeling some affection for them. They were
the ones who enlivened the whole table by their superiority in every respect to the others. Those men were
really remarkable, and seemed in some sense reflections
of Leoni. They had that sort of family resemblance,
that conformity of ideas and language which had impressed me the first day. There was an indefinable air
of subtlety and distinction, which was lacking even in
the most distinguished of the others. Their glances were
more penetrating, their replies more prompt, their self-
possession more lordly, their reckless extravagance in
better taste. Each one of them exerted a sort of moral
authority over a portion of the new-comers. They acted

as their models and guides, at first in small matters, afterward in greater ones. Leoni was the soul of the whole body, the superior chief who was the mentor of that brilliant masculine coterie, in style, tone, dissipation and extravagance.

This species of empire pleased him, and I was not surprised at it. I had seen him reign even more openly at Brussels, and I had shared his pride and his glory; but our happy life at the chalet had taught me the secret of purer, more private joys. I regretted that life, and could not refrain from saying so.

"And so do I," said he. "I regret those months of pure delight, superior to all the empty vanities of society; but God did not choose to change the succession of the seasons for us. There is no eternal happiness any more than there is perpetual spring. It is a law of nature which we cannot escape. Be sure that everything is ordered for the best in this wicked world. The strength of a man's heart is no greater than the duration of the blessings of life. Let us submit; let us bend our necks. The flowers droop, wither and are born again every year. The human heart can renew itself like a flower, when it knows its own strength and does not bloom to the bursting point. Six months of unalloyed felicity was a tremendous allowance, my dear; we should have died of too much happiness if that had continued, or else we should have abused it. Destiny bids us come down from our ethereal peaks and breathe a less pure atmosphere in cities. Let us bow to the necessity and believe that it is well for us. When the fine weather returns again, we will return to our mountains. We shall be the more eager to find there all the pleasures of which we are deprived here; we shall better appreciate the value of our peaceful privacy; and that season of love and delight,

16

which the hardships of the winter would have spoiled for us, will come again even lovelier than last year."

"Oh, yes," said I, embracing him, "we will return to Switzerland! How good you are to want to do it and to promise me that you will! But tell me, Leoni, can we not live more simply and more by ourselves here? We see each other now only through the fumes of punch; we speak to each other only amid songs and laughter. Why have we so many friends? Are we not enough for each other?"

"Why, Juliette," he replied, "angels are children, and you are both. You do not know that love is the function of the noblest faculties of the mind, and that we must take care of those faculties as of the apple of one's eye. You do not know, little girl, what your own heart is. Dear, sensitive, confiding creature that you are, you believe that it is an inexhaustible fountain of love; but the sun itself is not eternal. You do not know that the heart becomes tired like the body, and that it must be treated with the same care. Trust to me, Juliette; let me keep the sacred fire alight in your heart. It is my interest to preserve your love, to prevent you from squandering it too rapidly. All women are like you; they are in such a hurry to love that they suddenly cease to love, and do not know why."

"Bad boy," I said, "are these the things you said to me in the evenings on the mountain? Did you urge me not to love you too much? did you think that I was capable of becoming weary of loving you?"

"No, my angel," Leoni replied, kissing my hands, "nor do I think it now. But listen to my experience: external things exert upon our most secret feelings an influence against which the strongest contend in vain. In our valley, surrounded by pure air, by natural per-

fumes and melodies, we might well be and were certain
to be all love, all poesy, all enthusiasm : but remember
that, even while we were there, I was sparing of that
enthusiasm, which is so easy to lose, so impossible to
find again when it is lost; remember our rainy days, when
I was more or less harsh with you in forcing you to keep
your mind occupied, in order to save you from reflection
and the melancholy which is its inevitable consequence.
Be sure that too frequent examination of oneself and
others is the most dangerous of occupations. We must
shake off the selfish craving which impels us to be forever
searching our hearts and the hearts of those who love
us, like a foolish husbandman who exhausts the soil by
dint of calling on it to produce beyond its capacity. We
must know how to be unemotional and frivolous at times ;
such periods of distraction are dangerous only to weak
and indolent hearts. An ardent heart ought to seek them
in order not to consume itself; it is always rich enough.
A word, a glance, is sufficient to send a thrill through it
in the midst of the eddying whirl which carries it away,
and to bring it back more ardent and more loving to the
consciousness of its passion. Here, you see, we must
have excitement and variety; these great palaces are
beautiful, but they are melancholy. The sea moss clings
to their feet, and the limpid water in which they are reflected is often laden with vapors which fall in tears.
This magnificence is severe, and these marks of nobility
which please you are simply a long succession of epitaphs
and tombs which we must decorate with flowers. We
must fill with living beings this echoing mansion, where
your footsteps would frighten you if you were alone ; we
must throw money from the window to this populace
which has no other bed than the ice-covered parapets of
the bridges, so that the spectacle of its misery may not

make us sad amid our well-being. Allow yourself to be
cheered by our laughter and lulled to sleep by our
songs; be good and do not worry; I will undertake to
arrange your life and make it pleasant to you, even if I
am unable to make it intoxicating. Be my wife and my
mistress at Venice ; you shall be my angel and my nymph
again among the glaciers of Switzerland."

XI

By such speeches he allayed my anxiety and led me,
fascinated and confiding, to the brink of the abyss. I
thanked him lovingly for the trouble he took to persuade
me, when he could make me obey with a sign. We embraced affectionately and returned to the salon where our
friends awaited us to part us.

However, as the days succeeded one another, Leoni
did not take the same trouble to reconcile me to them.
He paid less attention to my growing discontent, and
when I mentioned it to him, he argued with me less
gently. One day indeed he was short with me and bitter ;
I saw that I offended him ; I determined to complain no
more ; but I began to suffer really and to be genuinely
unhappy. I waited with resignation until Leoni snatched
a few moments to come to me. To be sure he was so
kind and loving at those times that I deemed myself
foolish and cowardly to have suffered so. My courage
and my confidence would revive for a few days; but
those days of encouragement became more and more in-
frequent. Leoni, seeing that I was meek and submis-

sive, still treated me with consideration; but he no longer noticed my melancholy. Ennui devoured me, Venice
became hateful to me; its canals, its gondolas, its sky,
everything about it was distasteful. During the nights
of card-playing I wandered alone on the terrace at the
top of the house; I shed bitter tears; I recalled my home,
my heedless youth, my kind, foolish mother, my poor
father, so loving and so good-natured, and even my aunt,
with her petty worries and her long sermons. It seemed
to me that I was really homesick, that I longed to fly, to
go home and throw myself at my parents' feet, to forget
Leoni forever. But if a window opened below me, if
Leoni, weary of the game and the heat, came out on the
balcony to breathe the fresh air from the canal, I would
lean over the rail to look at him, and my heart would
beat as during the first days of my passion, when he
crossed the threshold of my father's house; if the moon
shone upon him and enabled me to distinguish that noble
figure beneath the rich fancy costume that he always
wore in his own palace, I would thrill with pride and
pleasure as on the evening that he led me into that ball-
room from which we went forth never to return; if his
melodious voice, murmuring a measure from some song,
rebounded from the resonant marbles of Venice and rose
to my ears, I would feel the tears flowing down my
cheeks, as on those evenings among the mountains when
he sang me a ballad composed for me in the morning.

A few words which I overheard from the mouth of one
of his friends increased my depression and my disgust to
an intolerable degree. Among Leoni's twelve intimate
associates, the Vicomte de Chalm, who called himself an
émigré Frenchman, was the one whose attentions were
most offensive to me. He was the oldest of them all,
and perhaps the cleverest; but underneath his exquisite

manners I detected a sort of cynicism which often revolted me. He was satirical, cold-blooded and insolent;
furthermore, he was a man without morals and without
heart; but I knew nothing of that, and he displeased
me, apart from that. One evening when I was on the
balcony, hidden from him by the silk curtains, I heard
him say to the Venetian marquis: "Why, where's Juliette?"—That mode of speaking of me brought the blood
to my cheeks; I kept perfectly still and listened.—"I
don't know," the Venetian replied. "Why, are you so
much in love with her?"—"Not too much," was the
reply, "but enough."—"And Leoni?"—"Leoni will
turn her over to me one of these days."—"What! his
own wife?"—"Nonsense, marquis! are you mad?" replied the viscount; "she is a girl he seduced at Brussels; when he has had enough of her, and that will be
before long, I will gladly take charge of her. If you want
her next after me, marquis, put your name down."—
"Many thanks," replied the marquis; "I know how you
deprave women, and I should be afraid to succeed you."

I heard no more; I leaned over the balustrade half-
dead, and, hiding my face in my shawl, wept with rage
and shame.

That same night I called Leoni into my room, and demanded satisfaction for the way I was treated by his
friends. He took the insult with a coolness which dealt
my heart a mortal blow.—"You are a little fool," he
said to me; "you don't know what men are; their
thoughts are indiscreet and their words still more so;
the rakes are the best of them. A strong woman should
laugh at their airs instead of losing her temper."

I fell upon a chair and burst into tears, crying;—"O
mother! mother! how low has your daughter fallen!"

Leoni exerted himself to soothe me, and succeeded only

too quickly. He knelt at my feet, kissed my hands and my arms, implored me to treat with scorn a foolish remark and to think of nothing but him and his love.

"Alas!" said I, "what am I to think when your friends flatter themselves that they can pick me up as they do your old pipes when you want them no longer."

"Juliette," he replied, "wounded pride makes you bitter and unjust. I have been a libertine, as you know; I have often told you of my youthful disorders; but I thought that I had purified myself in the air of our valley. My friends are still living the life that I used to lead; they know nothing of the six months we passed in Switzerland; they could never understand them. But ought you to misinterpret and forget them?"

I begged his pardon, I shed sweeter tears on his brow and his beautiful hair; I strove to forget the uncomfortable impression I had received. I flattered myself moreover that he would make his friends understand that I was not a kept mistress and that they must respect me; but he either did not choose to do it or did not think of it, for on the next and following days I saw that Monsieur de Chalm's eyes followed me and solicited me with revolting insolence.

I was in despair, but I did not know which way to turn to avoid the evils into which I had plunged. I was too proud to be happy, and loved Leoni too dearly to leave him.

One evening I had gone into the salon to get a book I had left on the piano. Leoni was surrounded by a select party of his friends; they were grouped around the tea table at the end of the room, which was dimly lighted, and did not notice my presence. The viscount seemed to be in one of his wickedest teasing moods.

"Baron Leone de Leoni," he said in a dry, mocking

voice, "do you know, my dear fellow, that you are getting in very deep?"

"What do you mean?" rejoined Leoni, "I have no debts at Venice yet."

"But you soon will have."

"I hope so," retorted Leoni with the utmost tranquillity.

"*Vive Dieu!*" said the viscount, "you are the first of men when it comes to ruining yourself; half a million in three months! do you know that's running a very pretty rig?"

Surprise had nailed me to my place; motionless and holding my breath, I awaited the end of this strange conversation.

"Half a million?" echoed the Venetian marquis indifferently.

"Yes," said Chalm, "Thaddeus the Jew advanced him five hundred thousand francs at the beginning of the winter."

"That's doing very well," said the marquis. "Have you paid the rent of your ancestral palace, Leoni?"

"*Parbleu!* yes, in advance," said Chalm; "would they have let it to him otherwise?"

"What do you expect to do when you have nothing left?" queried another of Leoni's trusty friends.

"Run in debt," replied Leoni with imperturbable tranquillity.

"That's easier than to find Jews who will leave you at peace for three months," said the viscount. "What will you do when your creditors take you by the collar?"

"I will take a pretty little boat," replied Leoni with a smile.

"Good! and go to Trieste?"

"No, that is too near; to Palermo, I have never been there."

"But when you arrive anywhere," said the marquis, "you must cut something of a figure for a few days."

"Providence will provide for that," said Leoni, "she is the mother of the audacious."

"But not of the indolent," said Chalm, "and I know nobody on earth more indolent than you. What the devil did you do in Switzerland with your infanta for six months?"

"Silence on that subject!" retorted Leoni; "I loved her, and I'll throw my glass at the head of any man who sees anything to laugh at in that."

"Leoni, you drink too much," observed another of his friends.

"Perhaps so, but I have said what I have said."

The viscount didn't take up this species of challenge, and the marquis made haste to change the conversation.

"Why, in God's name, aren't you playing?" he asked Leoni.

"*Ventre-Dieu!* I play every day to oblige you, although I detest gambling; you will make a fool of me with your cards and your dice, and your pockets like the cask of the Danaides, and your insatiable hands! You are nothing but a parcel of fools, the whole of you. When you have made a hit, instead of taking a rest and enjoying life like true sybarites, you keep at it until you have spoiled your luck."

"Luck, luck!" said the marquis, "everyone knows what luck is."

"Many thanks!" said Leoni, "I no longer care to know; I was too thoroughly currycombed at Paris.

When I think that there is one man, whom may God in his mercy consign to all the devils——!"

"Well?" said the viscount.

"A man," said the marquis, "of whom we must rid ourselves at any cost, if we wish to enjoy liberty again on this earth. But, patience, there are two of us against him."

"Never fear," said Leoni, "I have not so far forgotten the old customs of the country that I don't know how to clear my path of the man who stands in my way. Except for my devil of a love-affair, which filled my brain, I had a fine chance in Brussels."

"You?" said the marquis; "you never did anything in that line, and you will never have the courage."

"Courage?" cried Leoni, half-rising, with flashing eyes.

"No extravagance," replied the marquis, with that horrifying sang-froid which they all had. "Let us understand each other. You have courage to kill a bear or a wild boar, but you have too many sentimental and philosophical ideas in your head to kill a man."

"That may be," said Leoni, resuming his seat, "but I am not sure."

"You don't mean to play at Palermo, then?" said the viscount.

"To the devil with your gambling! If I could get up a passion for something—hunting, or a horse, or an olive-skinned Calabrian—I would go next summer, and shut myself up in the Abruzzi and pass a few more months forgetting you all."

"Rekindle your passion for Juliette," said the viscount, with a sneer.

"I will not rekindle my passion for Juliette," replied

Leoni, angrily, "but I will strike you if you mention her
name again."

"We must make him drink some tea," said the viscount, "he's dead drunk."

"Come, come, Leoni," cried the marquis, grasping
his arm, "you treat us horribly to-night. What's the
matter with you, in God's name? Are we no longer
friends? do you doubt us? Speak."

"No, I don't doubt you," said Leoni; "you have
given me back as much as I took from you. I know
what you are worth; good and bad, I judge you all,
without prejudice or prepossession."

"Ah! I should like to hear your judgment!" said the
viscount, between his teeth.

"Come, come! more punch! more punch!" cried
the other guests. "There's no possibility of any more
fun unless we drink Chalm and Leoni under the table.
They have reached the stage of nervous spasms; let's
put them in a trance."

"Yes, my friends, my very dear friends!" cried Leoni,
"punch! friendship! life—a jolly life! The deuce take
the cards! they are what make me ugly. Here's to
drunkenness! Here's to the ladies! Here's to sloth,
tobacco, music and money! Here's to the young maids
and old countesses! Here's to the devil! Here's to
love! Here's to all that makes one live! Everything
is good when one is well enough constituted to make the
most of it and enjoy it."

They all rose, shouting a drinking song. I fled; I ran
upstairs with the frenzy of one who thinks herself pursued, and fell in a swoon on my bedroom floor.

XII

The next morning they found me lying on the floor, as stiff and cold as a corpse; I had brain fever. I believe that Leoni was attentive to me; it seemed to me that I saw him frequently at my bedside, but I had only a vague memory of it. After three days I was out of danger. Then Leoni came from time to time to inquire for me, and to pass part of the afternoon with me. He left the palace every evening at six o'clock, and did not return until next morning. That fact I learned later.

Of all that I had heard I had clearly understood but one thing, which was the cause of my despair: it was that Leoni no longer loved me. Until then I had always refused to believe it, although his conduct should have made it clear to me. I resolved to contribute no farther to his ruin, and not to abuse a remnant of compassion and generosity which led him to continue to show me some consideration. I sent for him as soon as I felt strong enough to endure the interview, and told him what I had heard him say about me in the midst of the revel; I kept silence as to all the rest. I could not see clearly in that confused mass of infamous things which the remarks of his friends had caused me to suspect; I did not choose to understand them. Moreover, I was ready to consent to everything: to desertion, despair and death.

I told him that I had decided to go away in a week, and that I would accept nothing from him thenceforth. I had kept my father's pin; by selling it I could obtain much more than I needed to return to Brussels.

The courage with which I spoke, and which the fever doubtless assisted, dealt Leoni an unexpected blow. He said nothing, but paced the floor excitedly; then he began to sob and cry, and fell, gasping for breath, on a chair. Dismayed by his apparent condition, I left my reclining chair in spite of myself, and went to him with an air of solicitude. Thereupon he seized me in his arms and, pressing me frantically to his breast, cried:

" No, no! you shall not leave me; I will never consent to it; if your pride, perfectly just and legitimate as it is, will not let you yield, I will lie at your feet, across this doorway, and I will kill myself if you step over me. No, you shall not go, for I love you passionately; you are the only woman in the world whom I have ever been able to respect and admire after possessing her for six months. What I said was nonsense, and an infamous lie; you do not know, Juliette, oh! you do not know all my misfortunes! you do not know to what I am condemned by the society of a coterie of abandoned men, to what I am impelled by a soul of brass, fire, gold and mud, which I received from heaven and hell in concert! If you will not love me any longer, then I will live no longer. What have I not done, what have I not sacrificed, what faculties have I not debased, to retain my hold upon this execrable life, made execrable by them! What mocking demon is confined in my brain to make me still find attraction in this life at times, and shatter the most sacred ties to plunge into it still deeper? Ah! it is time to have done with it. Since I was born, I have known but one really beautiful, really pure time, and that was when I possessed and adored you. That purged me of all my wickedness, and I should have remained in the chalet under the snow; I should have died at peace with you, with God and with myself, whereas here I am ruined in your eyes and my own. Juliette, Juliette! mercy, pardon! I feel that my heart will break if you abandon me. I am young still; I want to live, to be happy, and I never shall be, except with you. Will you punish me with death for a blasphemous word that escaped my lips when I was intoxicated? Do you believe what I said? can you believe it? Oh! how I suffer! how I have suffered for a fortnight! I have secrets which burn my vitals; if only I could tell them to you!—but you would never be able to listen to the end."

"I know them," I cried; "and if you loved me, I would care nothing for all the rest."

"You know them!" he exclaimed with an air of bewilderment; "you know them? What do you know?"

"I know that you are ruined, that this palace is not yours, that you have squandered an enormous sum in three months; I know that you have become accustomed to this adventurous life and these dissipated habits. I do not know how you reconstruct your fortune so quickly or how you throw it away; I fancy that gambling is your ruin and your resource; I believe that you have about you a deplorable circle of friends, and that you are struggling against shockingly bad advice; I believe that you are on the brink of a precipice, but that you can still avoid it."

"Well, yes, that is all true," he cried; "you know everything! and you will forgive me?"

"If I had not lost your love," I replied, "I should not consider it a loss to leave this palace, this luxury and this society, all of which are hateful to me. However poor we may be, we can always live as we lived in our chalet—there, or somewhere else, if you are tired of Switzerland. If you still loved me, you would not be ruined; for you would think neither of gambling nor of

intemperance, nor of any of the passions which you com-
memorated in an infernal toast; if you loved me, you
would pay what you owe with what you have left, and
we would go and bury ourselves and love each other in
some secluded spot where I would quickly forget what I
have learned, where I would never remind you of it,
where I could not suffer because of it—if you loved me!''

"Oh! I do love you, I do love you!" he cried; "let
us go! let us fly, save me! Be my benefactress, my
angel, as you have always been! Come, and forgive
me!''

He threw himself at my feet and all that the most fervent passion can dictate, he said to me with so much
warmth that I believed it—and I shall always believe it.
Leoni deceived me, degraded me, and loved me at the
same time.

One day, to evade the keen reproaches that I heaped
upon him, he tried to rehabilitate the passion of gambling.

"Gambling," he said, with the specious eloquence
which had only too much power over me, "is a passion
much more energetic than love. More fruitful in terrible
dramas, it is more intoxicating, more heroic in the acts
which combine to attain its end. I must say it, alas!
that while that end is vile in appearance, the ardor is irresistible, the audacity is sublime, the sacrifices are blind
and unlimited. You must know, Juliette, that women
never inspire such passions. Gold has a power superior
to theirs. In strength, in courage, in devotion, in perse-
verance, love, compared with the gambler's stake, is only
a feeble child whose efforts are deserving of pity. How
many men have you seen sacrifice to a mistress that in-
estimable treasure, that priceless necessity, that condition of existence without which we feel that existence is
unendurable—*honor?* I have known very few whose

devotion goes beyond the sacrifice of life. Every day the
gambler sacrifices his honor and lives on. The gambler
is keen, he is stoical, he takes his triumph coolly, he
takes his downfall coolly; he passes in a few hours from
the lowest ranks of society to the highest; in a few hours
more he goes down again to his starting-point, and all
without change of attitude or expression. In a few hours,
without leaving the spot to which his demon chains him,
he incurs all the vicissitudes of life, he passes through all
the phases of fortune which represent the different social
conditions. By turns king and beggar, he climbs the long
ladder at a single stride, always calm, always self-con-
trolled, always sustained by his sturdy ambition, always
spurred on by the intense thirst that consumes him.
What will he be an hour hence? prince or slave? How
will he come forth from that den? stripped naked or bent
beneath the weight of gold? What does it matter? He
will return to-morrow to remake his fortune, to lose it or
to triple it. The one thing impossible for him is repose;
he is like the storm bird that cannot live without rag-
ing winds and an angry sea. He is accused of loving
gold! he loves it so little that he throws it away by the
handful. That gift of hell is powerless to benefit him or
satisfy his craving. He is no sooner rich than he is in
great haste to be ruined in order to enjoy that nerve-
racking, terrible emotion without which life is tasteless to
him. What is gold in his eyes? Less in itself than
grains of sand in yours. But gold is to him an emblem
of the blessings and the evils which he seeks and defies.
Gold is his plaything, his enemy, his God, his dream, his
demon, his mistress, his poesy: it is the ghost which
haunts him, which he attacks, grasps, and then allows to
escape, that he may have the pleasure of renewing the
struggle and of engaging once more in a hand-to-hand

conflict with destiny. It is magnificent, I tell you ! It is absurd, to be sure, and should be condemned, because energy thus employed is of no advantage to society, because the man who expends his strength for such an end robs his fellow-men of all the good he might have done, them with less selfishness ; but when you condemn him, do not despise him, ye narrow-minded creatures who are capable of neither good nor evil ; do not gaze with dismay at the colossus of will-power, struggling thus on a tempestuous sea for the sole purpose of exerting his strength and forcing the sea back. His selfishness leads him into the midst of fatigues and dangers, as yours binds you down to patient, hard-working occupations. How many men in the whole world can you think of who work for their country without thinking of themselves ? He voluntarily isolates himself, sets himself apart; he stakes his present, his repose, his honor. He dooms himself to suffering, to fatigue. Deplore his error if you will, but do not compare yourself with him, in the pride of your heart, in order to glorify yourself at his expense. Let his fatal example serve simply to console you for your own harmless nullity."

"O heaven!" I replied, "upon what sophistries your heart feeds, or else how weak my mind must be ! What! the gambler is not despicable, you say ? O Leoni, why, having so much strength of mind, have you not employed it in overcoming yourself in the interest of your fellow-men ?"

"Apparently, because I have misunderstood life," he replied in a bitter, ironical tone. "Because, instead of appearing on a sumptuously appointed stage, I appeared in an open-air theatre ; because, instead of spending my time declaiming specious moral apothegms on the stage of society and playing heroic rôles, I amused myself by

17

performing feats of strength and risking my life on a tight-rope, in order to give full play to the strength of my muscles. And even that comparison amounts to nothing: the tight-rope dancer has his vanity as well as the tragedian or the philanthropic orator. The gambler has none; he is neither admired nor applauded nor envied. His triumphs are so short-lived and so hazardous that it is hardly worth while to speak of them. On the other hand, society condemns him, the common herd despises him, especially on the days when he has lost. All his charlatanism consists in showing a bold front, in falling manfully before a group of selfish creatures who do not even look at him, they are so engrossed by their own mental struggles! If in his swift hours of good luck he finds some enjoyment in gratifying the commonplace vanities of luxury, it is a very brief tribute that he pays to human weaknesses. Ere long he will go and sacrifice remorselessly those childish joys of an instant to the devouring activity of his mind, to that infernal fever which does not permit him to live for one whole day as other men live. Vanity in him! Why, he has not the time for it, he has something else to do! Has he not his heart to torture, his brain to overturn, his blood to drink, his flesh to torment, his gold to lose, his life to endanger, to reconstruct, to pull down, to wrench, to tear in pieces, to risk altogether, to reconquer, bit by bit, to put in his purse, to toss on the table every moment? Ask the sailor if he can live on shore, the bird if he can do without his wings, man's heart if it can do without emotions. The gambler then is not criminal in himself; it is always his social position that makes him so, his family, whom he ruins or dishonors. But suppose him to be like me, alone in the world, without attachments, without kindred near enough in degree to be taken into account, free, thrown on his own resources, satiated or deceived in love, as I have so often been, and you will pity his error, you will regret for his sake that he was born with a sanguine and vain rather than with a bilious and reserved temperament. How do you argue that the gambler is in the same category as brigands and filibusters? Ask governments why they derive a part of their revenues from such a shameful source? They alone are guilty of offering those terrible temptations to restlessness, those deplorable resources to despair. But although love of gambling is not in itself so degrading as the majority of other passions, it is the most dangerous of all, the keenest, the most irresistible, and attended by the most wretched consequences. It is almost impossible for the gambler not to dishonor himself for a few years. As for myself," he added, with a gloomier manner and in a less vibrant voice, "after enduring for a long time this life of torture and convulsions with the chivalrous heroism which was the foundation of my character, I allowed myself to be corrupted at last; that is to say, my strength being gradually exhausted by this constant conflict, I lost the stoical courage with which I had accepted reverses, endured the privations of ghastly poverty, recommenced the building of my fortune, sometimes with a single sou, waited, hoped, advanced warily and step by step, sacrificing a whole month to repair the losses of a single day. Such was my life for a long while. But at last, weary of suffering, I began to seek outside of my own will, outside of my virtue,—for it must be admitted that the gambler has a virtue of his own,— the means of regaining more quickly what I had lost; I borrowed and from that moment I was lost myself. At first a man suffers cruelly when he finds himself in an indelicate position; but eventually he gets used to it, as to everything else, becomes numb and indifferent. I did

as all gamblers and spendthrifts do; I became dangerous
and harmful to my friends. I heaped upon their heads
the evils which I had for a long time bravely borne on my
own. It was very culpable ; I risked my own honor,
then the honor and the lives of my nearest and dearest,
as I had risked my money. There is this that is horrible
about gambling, that it gives you none of those lessons
which it is impossible to forget. It is always there,
beckoning to you! That inexhaustible pile of gold is
always before your eyes. It follows you about, it coaxes
you, it bids you hope, and sometimes it keeps its promises, restores your courage, re-establishes your credit,
seems to postpone dishonor again ; but dishonor is con-
summated the moment that honor is voluntarily put in
peril."

Here Leoni hung his head and relapsed into moody
silence; the confession that perhaps he had intended to
make to me died on his lips. I saw by his shame and
his depression that it was quite useless to expose the so-
phistical arguments of his disordered brain ; his conscience had already undertaken that task.

"Listen to me," he said, when we were reconciled.
"To-morrow I close the house to all my friends and go
to Milan, where I have to collect a considerable sum that
is still due me. While I am gone, take good care of
yourself, get well, arrange all the claims of our creditors, and make preparations for our departure. In a week,
or a fortnight at most, I will return and pay our debts,
take you away, and live with you wherever you
choose, forever."

I believed all he said ; I consented to everything. He
went away and the house was closed. I did not wait
until I was entirely well before I set at work to put
everything in order and to inspect the tradesmen's bills.

I hoped that Leoni would write me on arriving at Milan
as he had promised. It was more than a week before I
heard from him. He wrote me at last that he was sure
of collecting much more money than he owed, but that
he would be obliged to remain away three weeks instead
of two. I resigned myself to wait. At the end of three
weeks another letter informed me that he was compelled
to wait for his money until the end of the month. I was
discouraged. Alone in that vast palace, where, in order
to avoid the insolent attentions of Leoni's boon-com-
panions, I was obliged to conceal myself, to lower my
curtains and sustain a sort of siege, consumed with anxiety, ill and weak, abandoned to the blackest thoughts
and to all the remorse which the sting of unhappiness
arouses, I was tempted many times to put an end to my
miserable life.

But I was not at the end of my sufferings.

XIII

One morning, when I thought that I was alone in the
great salon, where I sat with an open book on my knees,
never thinking of glancing at it, I heard a noise near me,
and throwing off my lethargy, I saw the hateful face of
Vicomte de Chalm. I uttered an exclamation, and was
about to turn him out of doors, when he apologized pro-
fusely with an air that was at once respectful and ironical, and I was at a loss for a reply. He said that he had
forced my door by virtue of the authority contained in
a letter from Leoni, who had specially instructed him to

come to inquire about my health and report to him. I put no faith in this pretext, and was on the point of telling him so. He gave me no time, however, but began to talk himself with such impudent self-possession, that it would have been impossible for me to turn him out unless by calling my servants. He had resolved to take no hints.

"I see, madame," he said to me, with a hypocritical air of friendly interest, "that you are aware of the baron's unfortunate position. Be assured that my slender resources are at his disposal; unluckily they amount to very little in the way of satisfying the prodigality of such a magnificent character. What consoles me is that he is brave, enterprising and ingenious. He has rebuilt his fortune several times; he will do it again. But you will have to suffer, madame; you who are so young and delicate, so worthy of a happier lot! It is on your account that I am profoundly distressed by Leoni's follies, and by all those he has still to commit before he obtains what he needs. Poverty is a horrible thing at your age, and when one has always lived in luxury——"

I interrupted him abruptly, for I fancied that I could see what he was coming to with his insulting compassion. I did not yet realize that creature's baseness.

Divining my suspicion, he made haste to destroy it. He gave me to understand, with all the courtesy that his cold and cunning tongue could command, that he considered himself too old and too poor to offer me his support, but that an immensely wealthy young English lord, whom he had introduced to me and who had called on me several times, entrusted to him the honorable mission of tempting me by magnificent promises. I had not the strength to reply to that insult. I was so weak and so prostrated that I began to weep, without speaking. The

infamous Chalm thought that I was wavering, and, in
order to hasten my decision, informed me that Leoni
would not return to Venice, that he was fast bound at
the feet of Princess Zagorolo, and that he had given him
full power to conclude this affair with me.

Indignation at last restored the presence of mind which
I needed to overwhelm that man with contempt and ob-
loquy. ·But he soon recovered from his confusion.

"I see, madame," he said, "that your youth and in-
nocence have been cruelly abused, and I am incapable
of returning hatred for hatred, for you misunderstand
me, and therefore accuse me, whereas I know and esteem you. I will listen to your reproaches and your
insults with all the stoicism which genuine devotion
should have at its command, and then I will tell you into
what an abyss you have fallen and from what depths of
degradation I desire to rescue you."

He said this with such emphasis and so calmly that my
credulous nature was in a measure subjugated. For an
instant I thought that I had, perhaps, misjudged a sincere
friend in the mental disturbance caused by my misfortunes. Fascinated by the impudent serenity of his
features, I forgot the disgusting words I had heard him
use, and I gave him time to speak. He saw that he
must make the most of that moment of hesitation and
weakness, and he made haste to give me information
concerning Leoni that bore the stamp of hateful truth.

"I admire," he said, "the way in which your easily
persuaded and confiding heart has clung so long to such
a character. It is true that nature has endowed him with
irresistible fascinations, and that he is extraordinarily
skilful in concealing his villainy and assuming the out-
ward appearance of loyalty. All the cities in Europe
know him for a delightful rake. Only a very few per-

sons in Italy know that he is capable of any villainy to gratify his innumerable whims. To-day you will see him take Lovelace for his model, to-morrow the shepherd Fido. As he is something of a poet, he is capable of receiving all sorts of impressions, of understanding and mimicking all the virtues, of studying and playing all varieties of rôles. He believes that he really feels all that he imitates, and sometimes he identifies himself so thoroughly with the character he has chosen, that he feels its passions and grasps its grandeur. But, as he is vile and corrupt at bottom, as there is nothing in him save affectation and caprice, vice suddenly springs to life in his blood, the tedium of his hypocrisy drives him into habits directly contrary to those which seemed natural to him. They who have seen him only in one of his deceptive disguises are amazed and think he has gone mad; they who know that it is his nature to be true in nothing, smile and wait quietly for some fresh invention."

Although this shocking portrait revolted me so that I was almost suffocated, yet it seemed to me that I saw in it some shafts of blinding light. I was struck dumb, my nerves contracted. I looked at Chalm with a terror-stricken expression; he congratulated himself on his success and continued:

" This revelation of his character surprises you; if you had had more experience, my dear lady, you would know that such a character is very common in the world. To have it to perfection, one must have a very superior mind; and the reason that many fools do not assume it is that they are incapable of sustaining it. You will notice that a vain man of moderate parts will almost always shut himself up in a sort of obstinacy which he deems peculiar to himself and which consoles him for another's success. He will admit that he is less brilliant, but will claim that he is more reliable and more useful. The world is inhabited by none but intolerable idiots and dangerous madmen. Everything considered, I prefer the latter; I have prudence enough to protect myself from them and tolerance enough to be amused by them. It is much better to laugh with a spiteful buffoon than to yawn with a tiresome virtuous man. That is why you have seen me living on intimate terms with a man whom I neither like nor esteem. Moreover I was attracted to this house by your amiable manners, by your angelic sweetness; I felt a fatherly affection for you. Young Lord Edwards, who from his window saw that you passed many hours motionless and pensive on your balcony, confided to me the violent passion he has conceived for you. I introduced him here, frankly and earnestly hoping that you would remain no longer in the painful and humiliating position in which Leoni's desertion left you; I knew that Lord Edwards had a heart worthy of yours, and that he would make your life happy and honorable. I have come to-day to renew my efforts and to avow his love, which you have not chosen to understand."

I bit my handkerchief in my indignation; but, absorbed by one fixed idea, I rose and said to him with emphasis:

"You claim that Leoni has authorized you to make me these infamous propositions: prove it! yes, monsieur, prove it!"

And I shook his arm with convulsive force.

"*Parbleu!* my dear girl," the villain retorted with his hateful sang-froid, "it's very easy to prove. But how is it that you don't understand it? Leoni no longer loves you; he has another mistress."

"Prove it!" I repeated, thoroughly exasperated.

"In a moment, in a moment," said he. "Leoni is in

great need of money, and there are some women of a
certain age whose countenance may be advantageous."

"Prove to me all that you say," I cried, "or I turn you
out of the house instantly."

"Very well," he replied, not at all disconcerted; "but
let us make a bargain: if I have lied to you, I will leave
the house and never put my foot inside it again; but if I
told you the truth when I said that Leoni has authorized
me to speak to you about Lord Edwards, you will allow
me to come again this evening with him."

As he spoke he took from his pocket a letter, on the
envelope of which I recognized Leoni's handwriting.

"Yes!" I cried, carried away by the irresistible desire
to know my fate; "yes, I promise."

The marquis slowly unfolded the letter and handed it
to me. I read:

"MY DEAR VISCOUNT,

"Although you often cause me fits of anger in which I
would gladly strangle you, I believe that you are really
my friend and that your offers of service are sincere.
However, I will not take advantage of them. I have
something better than that, and my affairs are going on
famously once more. The only thing that embarrasses
me and frightens me is Juliette. You are right: the moment that she knows, she will upset my plans. But
what am I to do? I have the most idiotic and invincible
attachment for her. Her despair takes away all my
strength. I cannot see her weep without falling at her
feet. You think that she will allow herself to be corrupted? No, you do not know her; she will never allow
herself to be persuaded by greed. But anger? you say.
Yes, that is more probable. What woman is there who
will not do from anger what she would not do for love?

Juliette is proud, I have become perfectly certain of that lately. If you tell her a little ill of me, if you give her to understand that I am unfaithful—perhaps!—But, great God! I cannot think of it without feeling as if my heart were being torn to pieces.—Try: if she yields, I will despise her and forget her; if she resists—why, then we will see. Whatever the result of your efforts, I have either a great calamity to dread or a great heartache to endure."

"Now," said the marquis when I had finished reading, "I am going to fetch Lord Edwards."

I hid my face in my hands and sat for a long time without moving or speaking. Then I suddenly hid the hateful letter in my bosom and rang violently.

"Let my maid pack a portmanteau in five minutes," I said to the servant, "and tell Beppo to bring the gondola."

"What do you mean to do, my dear child?" said the astonished viscount; "where do you propose to go?"

"To Lord Edwards, of course," I retorted with a bitter irony of which he did not understand the meaning. "Go and tell him," I added; "say that you have earned your pay and that I am flying to him."

He began to understand that I was frantic with rage and was jeering at him. He paused, uncertain what to do. I left the salon without another word, and went to put on my travelling dress. I came down again, attended by my maid, who carried the portmanteau. As I was stepping into the gondola, I felt that a trembling hand caught my cloak and held me back; I turned and saw Chalm, greatly disturbed and alarmed.

"Where in heaven's name are you going?" he said in an altered voice.

I was triumphant to have destroyed his sang-froid, the sang-froid of a villain, at last.

"I am going to Milan," I said, "and I am going to make you lose the two or three hundred sequins Lord Edwards has promised you."

"One moment," shouted the viscount furiously, "give me the letter or you shall not go."

"Beppo!" I cried, wild with anger and terror, darting toward the gondolier, "save me from this ruffian, he is breaking my arm!"

All Leoni's servants, finding me a mild mistress, were devoted to me. Beppo, a silent, resolute fellow, seized me about the waist and lifted me from the stairs. At the same time he pushed against the lowest step with his foot, and the gondola shot out into the canal just as he deposited me on the seat with marvellous dexterity and strength. Chalm was very near being dragged into the water. He disappeared, after giving me a look which was a vow of everlasting hatred and implacable revenge.

XIV

I reached Milan after travelling night and day without giving myself time to rest or reflect. I alighted at the inn which Leoni had given me as his address, and asked for him; they looked at me in amazement.

"He does not live here," the clerk replied. "He came here when he arrived and hired a small room where he put his luggage; but he only comes here in the morning to get his letters and be shaved; then he goes away."

"But where are his lodgings?" I asked.

I saw that the man looked at me with curiosity and

uncertainty, and, whether from a feeling of respect or of compassion, could not make up his mind to reply. I was discreet enough not to insist, and bade them take me to the room Leoni had hired.

"If you know where he can be found at this time of day," I said to the clerk, "send for him and say that his sister has arrived."

In about an hour Leoni appeared and held out his arms to embrace me.

"Wait a moment," I said, drawing back, "if you have deceived me hitherto, do not add another crime to those you have already committed against me. Here, look at this letter; did you write it? If somebody has imitated your handwriting, tell me quickly, for I hope that it is so, and I am suffocating."

Leoni glanced at the letter and turned as pale as death.

"*Mon Dieu!*" I cried, "I hoped that I had been deceived! I came to you, almost certain of finding that you knew nothing of this infamy. I said to myself: ' He has done much that is bad, he has deceived me before; but, in spite of everything, he loves me. If it is true that I am an annoyance to him and that I stand in his way, he would have told me so when I felt the courage to leave him, barely a month ago; whereas he threw himself at my feet and implored me to remain. If he is ambitious and a schemer, he would not have kept me, for I have no fortune, and my love is of no advantage to him in any way. Why should he complain of my importunity now? He has but a word to say to send me away. He knows that I am proud; he need not fear my prayers or my reproaches. Why should he wish to degrade me?' "

I could not continue; a flood of tears choked my voice and arrested my words.

"Why should I wish to degrade you?" cried Leoni beside himself with emotion; "to spare my tattered conscience another cause for remorse! You cannot understand that, Juliette. It is easy to see that you have never committed a crime!"

He paused; I sank into a chair and we faced each other, equally overcome.

"Poor angel!" he cried at last, "did you deserve to be the companion and victim of such a knave as I am? What did you do to God before you were born, unfortunate child, that he should throw you into the arms of a villain who is killing you with shame and despair? Poor Juliette! poor Juliette!"

And in his turn he shed a torrent of tears.

"Very well," I said; "I came to hear your justification or my sentence. You are guilty, I forgive you and I go."

"Never say that again!" he cried vehemently. "Strike that word out of our interviews forever. When you intend to leave me, make your escape adroitly, so that I cannot prevent you; but so long as a drop of blood is left in my veins, I will not consent to it. You are my wife, you are my wife, you belong to me and I love you. I can kill you with grief, but I cannot let you go."

"I will accept the grief and death," I said, "if you tell me that you still love me."

"Yes, I love you, I love you!" he cried, with his usual transports. "I love no one but you, and I never shall be able to love any other!"

"Wretch! you lie," I said to him. "You have been paying court to the Princess Zagarolo."

"True, but I detest her."

"What!" I cried, in utter amazement. "Why do you follow her then? What shameful secrets are hidden beneath all these riddles ? Chalm tried to persuade me that a vile ambition bound you to that woman ; that she was old—that she paid you. Ah ! what things you make me say !''

"Do not believe these calumnies," said Leoni, "the princess is young and beautiful ; I am in love with her.''

"Very well," I said, with a profound sigh, "I would rather have you unfaithful than dishonored. Love her, love her dearly, for she is rich and you are poor! If you love her dearly, wealth and poverty will be mere words between you. I loved you so, and, although I had nothing to live on but what you gave me, I did not blush on that account ; now, I should debase myself and I should be unendurable to you. So let me go. Your obstinacy in keeping me here, just to kill me by torture, is both foolish and cruel.''

"That is true," said Leoni, gloomily. "Go! I am a villain to try to prevent you.''

He left the room with an air of desperation. I threw myself on my knees, I prayed to heaven to give me strength, I invoked the memory of my mother, and I rose to make once more my brief preparations for departure.

When my portmanteau was locked, I ordered post-horses for the same evening, and threw myself on the bed to wait. I was so overdone by fatigue and so prostrated by despair, that I felt, as I fell asleep, something resembling the peace of the grave.

After an hour's sleep, I was aroused by Leoni's passionate kisses.

"It is of no use for you to think of going away," he said; "it is beyond my strength. I have sent away your horses and had your trunk unpacked. I have been out walking alone in the country, and I have done my ut-

most to force myself to give you up. I resolved not to
bid you adieu. I went to the princess's and tried to persuade myself that I loved her; I hate her and I love you.
You must stay."

These constant agitations weakened my mind as well
as my body. I began to lose the faculty of reasoning;
evil and good, esteem and contempt became vague
sounds, words which I no longer cared to understand,
and which frightened me as much as if they were interminable columns of figures which I was told to add.
Leoni had thenceforth more than a moral influence
over me; he had a magnetic power which I could
not escape. His glance, his voice, his tears acted on my
nerves no less than on my heart. I was simply a ma-
chine turned any way at his pleasure.

I forgave him. I abandoned myself to his caresses; I
promised him whatever he chose. He told me that the
Princess Zagarolo, being a widow, had thought of marrying him; that the brief and trivial fancy he had had for
her had made her believe in his love; that she had foolishly compromised herself for him; and that he must
either spare her pride and cut loose from her gradually,
or have trouble with the whole family.

"If it were simply a matter of fighting with all her
brothers, cousins and uncles," he said, "I should
worry very little about it; but they will act as great
noblemen, denounce me as a *carbonaro*, and have
me thrown into prison, where I may have to wait ten
years before the authorities will deign to look into my
case."

I listened to all these absurd fables with the credulity
of a child. Leoni had never taken any part in politics,
but I was still fond of persuading myself that all that
was problematical in his life was connected with some

great enterprise of that kind.   I consented to pass for
his sister in the hotel, to go out seldom, and never
with him—in short, to leave him absolutely at liberty to
leave me at any moment at a nod from the princess.

XV

That life was perfectly frightful, but I endured it. The
tortures of jealousy had been unknown to me hitherto;
now they awoke, and I exhausted them all.   I spared
Leoni the tedium of combating them ; indeed I had not
enough strength left to express them. I resolved to allow
myself to die in silence ; I felt sick enough to hope for
death.   Ennui consumed me at Milan, even more than
at Venice ; I suffered more, and had less distraction.
Leoni lived openly with the Princess Zagarolo. He passed
the evening in her box at the play, or at some ball
with her.   He made his escape to come to see me for
an instant, then returned to sup with her, and did not
come back to the hotel until six o'clock in the morning.
He went to bed utterly exhausted and often in ill-humor.
He rose at noon, taciturn and distraught, and went to
drive with his mistress. I often saw them pass. Leoni
when with her had the same discreetly triumphant air,
the same coquettish bearing, the same fond and happy
expression that he once had with me ; now I had only
his complaints and a narrative of his vexations. To be
sure, I preferred to have him come to me careworn and
disgusted by his slavery, to being tranquil and indifferent, as sometimes happened.   It seemed at those
18

times that he had forgotten the love he had once had for
me and that which I still had for him. He found it altogether natural to confide to me the details of his intimacy
with another, and did not perceive that the smile on
my face as I listened to him was a mute convulsion of
pain.

One evening, at sunset, I was coming out of the cathedral, where I had prayed fervently to God to call me
back to him and to accept my sufferings in expiation of
my faults. I walked slowly through the magnificent
portal and leaned from time to time against a pillar, for I
was very weak. A slow fever was consuming me. The
excitement of prayer and the atmosphere of the church
had bathed me in a cold perspiration. I resembled a
spectre risen from the sepulchral vaults of the edifice to
look once more upon the last rays of the sun. A man
who had been following me for some time, without at-
tracting my attention particularly, spoke to me, and I
turned, without surprise or alarm, with the apathy of a
dying woman. I recognized Henryet.

Instantly, the memory of my home and my family
awoke in me with a violent throb. I forgot that young
man's strange behavior towards me, the terrible power
that he wielded over Leoni, his former love, which I had
welcomed so coldly, and the detestation I had felt for him
afterward. I thought only of my father and mother,
and eagerly offering him my hand, I overwhelmed him
with questions. He was in no hurry to reply, although
he seemed touched by my emotion and my eagerness.

"Are you alone here?" he said to me; "can I talk to
you without exposing you to any danger?"

"I am alone; no one here knows me or pays any
attention to me. Let us sit down on this stone bench,
for I am not well; and, for the love of heaven, tell me

about my parents! It is a whole year since I have heard
their names."

"Your parents!" said Henryet sadly; "there is one
of them who no longer weeps for you."

"My father is dead!" I cried, rising. Henryet did not
reply. I fell back, utterly crushed, on the bench, and
said under my breath: "My God, who wilt soon reunite
us, bid him forgive me!"

"Your mother," said Henryet, "was ill a long while.
Then she tried to find relief in society; but she had lost
her beauty with much weeping, and could find no consolation there."

"My father dead," I said, clasping my nerveless
hands, "my mother aged and heartbroken! What of my
aunt?"

"Your aunt tries to console your mother by proving
that you do not deserve her regrets; but your mother
will not listen to her and fades more and more every day
in solitude and weariness. And you, madame?"

Henryet uttered these last three words in a chilling
tone, in which, however, I could detect compassion beneath the apparent contempt.

"I, as you see, am dying."

He took my hand and tears came to his eyes.

"Poor girl!" he said to me; "it is not my fault. I
did all that I could to keep you from falling over the precipice, but you insisted."

"Do not speak of that," I said; "it is impossible for
me to discuss it with you. Tell me if my mother tried to
find me after my flight?"

"Your mother sought you, but not earnestly enough.
Poor woman! she was thunderstruck and lost her presence of mind. There is no vigor in the blood that you
inherit."

"That is true," said I indifferently. "We were all indolent and placid in my family. Did my mother hope that I would return?"

"She hoped so, foolishly and childishly. She still expects you and will expect you till her last breath."

I began to sob. Henryet let me weep without saying a word. I believe that he was weeping too. I wiped my eyes to ask him if my mother had been distressed by my dishonor, if she blushed for me, if she still dared to mention my name.

"She has it always on her lips," he replied. "She tells her grief to everybody; people are a little tired of the story now, and they smile when your mother begins to sob; or else they avoid her, saying: 'Here comes Madame Ruyter to tell us about her daughter's abduction again!'"

I listened to this without anger and said, raising my eyes to his:

"And do you despise me, Henryet?"

"I no longer love you or esteem you," he replied; "but I pity you and I am at your service. My purse is at your disposal. Do you wish to write to your mother? Would you like me to take you back to her? Speak, and do not fear to abuse me. I am not acting from affection but from a sense of duty. You have no idea, Juliette, how much sweeter life becomes to those who lay down rules for themselves and observe them."

I made no reply.

"Do you mean, then, to remain here alone and deserted? How long ago did *your husband* leave you?"

"He has not left me," I replied; "we live together; he objects to my going away, which I have long been planning to do, but which I no longer have the strength to think about."

I relapsed into silence; he gave me his arm as far as our hotel. I did not know when we arrived there. I fancied that I was leaning on Leoni's arm and I strove to conceal my sufferings and say nothing of them.

"Shall I come again to-morrow to learn your intentions?" said Henryet, as he left me at the door.

"Yes," I replied, not thinking that he might meet Leoni.

"At what time?"

"Whenever you choose," I answered with a dazed air.

He came the next day a few moments after Leoni had gone out. I had forgotten that I had given him permission to come, and I exhibited so much surprise that he was obliged to remind me. Thereupon, there came to my mind certain words I had overheard between Leoni and his companions, the meaning of which had hitherto been quite vague in my mind, but which seemed applicable to Henryet and to imply a threat of assassination. I shuddered as I reflected upon the danger to which I exposed him.

"Let us go out," I said in dismay; "you are not safe here."

He smiled, and his face expressed utter contempt for the danger I dreaded.

"Believe me," he said, as I seemed inclined to insist, "the man of whom you speak would not dare raise his hand against me, as he dares not even raise his eyes to mine."

I could not hear Leoni spoken of in that way. Despite all the wrongs he had done me, despite all his faults, he was still dearer to me than all the world. I requested Henryet not to refer to him in such terms before me.

"Overwhelm me with contempt," I said; "reproach me for being a heartless girl, utterly without pride; for having abandoned the best parents that ever lived; and for trampling on all the laws that are imposed upon my sex; I will take no offence, I will listen to you, weeping, and I will be none the less grateful to you for the offers of service you made me yesterday. But let me respect Leoni's name, it is the only treasure which, in the privacy of my heart, I can still oppose to the malediction of the world."

"Respect Leoni's name!" cried Henryet with a bitter laugh. "Poor woman! However, I will consent if you choose to start for Brussels! Go home and comfort your mother, return to the path of duty, and I promise to leave in peace the villain who has ruined you, and whom I could crush like a wisp of straw."

"Return to my mother!" I replied. "Oh! yes, my heart bids me do it every moment in the day; but my pride forbids me to return to Brussels. How should I be treated by all the women who were jealous of my splendor, and who rejoice now at my degradation?"

"I am afraid, Juliette," said he, "that that is not your strongest reason. Your mother has a country house where you can live with her far away from the hardhearted world. With your fortune you can live anywhere you please where your disgrace is not known, and where your beauty and your sweet nature would soon bring you new friends. But confess that you do not wish to leave Leoni."

"I do wish to," I replied, weeping, "but I cannot."

"Unfortunate, most unfortunate of women!" said Henryet sadly; "you are naturally good and beautiful, but you lack pride. Where noble pride is lacking, there is nothing to build upon. Poor weak creature! I pity you from the bottom of my soul, for you have profaned your heart, you have soiled it by contact with a vile heart, you have bent your neck under a hand stained with crime, you love a dastard! I ask myself how I could ever have loved you, but I also ask myself how I could fail to pity you now."

"Why, what in the name of heaven has Leoni done," I demanded, terrified and appalled by his manner and his language, " that you assume the right to speak of him in this way?"

"Do you doubt my right, madame? Do you wish me to tell you why Leoni, who is personally brave,—that is beyond question,—and who is the best swordsman that I know, has never thought fit to pick a quarrel with me, who never touched a sword in my life, and who drove him out of Paris with a word, out of Brussels with a glance?"

"That is inconceivable," I said, in dire distress.

" Is it possible that you don't know whose mistress you are?" continued Henryet earnestly; "has no one ever told you the marvellous adventures of Chevalier Leoni? have you never blushed for having been his accomplice and for having fled with a swindler after robbing your father's shop?"

I uttered a cry of anguish and hid my face in my hands; then I raised my head and exclaimed with all my strength:

"That is false! I never was guilty of such a despicable act! Leoni is no more capable of it than I am. We had not travelled forty leagues on the way to Geneva when Leoni stopped in the middle of the night, asked for a box, and put all the jewels in it to send them back to my father."

"Are you quite sure that he did that?" inquired Henryet with a contemptuous laugh.

"I am sure of it!" I cried; "I saw the box, I saw Leoni put the diamonds into it."

" And you are sure that the box didn't accompany you

all the rest of your journey ? you are sure that it wasn't
unpacked at Venice ? "

These words cast such a dazzling gleam of light into
my mind, that I could not avoid seeing what it disclosed.
I suddenly remembered what I had previously tried in
vain to remember : the first occasion on which my eyes
had made the acquaintance of that fatal box. At that
moment the three times that I had seen it were perfectly
clear in my mind and linked themselves together logically
to force me to an irresistible conclusion : the first, the night
we passed in the mysterious château, when I saw Leoni
put the diamonds in the box ; the second, the last night at
the Swiss chalet, when I saw Leoni mysteriously disinter
the treasure he had entrusted to the earth ; the third, the
second day of our stay in Venice, when I had found the
empty box and the diamond pin on the floor with the
packing material. The visit of Thaddeus the Jew, and
the five hundred thousand francs which, according to the
conversation I had overheard between Leoni and his
friends, had been advanced by him at the time of our
arrival in Venice, coincided perfectly with the memories
of that morning. I wrung my hands, then raised them
toward heaven and cried, speaking to myself :

" So everything is lost, even my mother's esteem ;
everything is poisoned, even the memory of Switzerland !
Those six months of love and happiness were devoted to
covering up a theft."

" And to eluding the pursuit of the police," added
Henryet.

" No ! no ! " I cried wildly, looking at him as if to
question him ; " he loved me ! it is certain that he loved
me ! I cannot think of that time without being absolutely
certain of his love. He was a thief who had stolen a maid
and a jewel-chest, and who loved them both."

Henryet shrugged his shoulders; I realized that I was wandering; and, struggling to recover my reason, I insisted upon knowing the explanation of the incredible power he possessed over Leoni.

"You want to know that?" he said. He reflected a moment, then continued: "I will tell you, I can safely tell you; indeed, it is impossible that you can have lived with him a year without suspecting it. He must have made dupes enough at Venice under your eyes."

"Made dupes! he! how so? Oh! be careful what you say, Henryet! he is burdened with accusations enough already."

"I believe that you are incapable as yet of being his accomplice, Juliette; but beware that you do not become so; be careful for your family's sake. I do not know to what point the impunity of a swindler's mistress extends."

"You are killing me with shame, monsieur; your words are cruel; pray complete your work and break my heart altogether by telling me what gives you the right of life and death, so to speak, over Leoni? Where have you known him? what do you know of his past life? I know nothing of it myself, alas! I have seen so many contradictory things about him that I no longer know whether he is rich or poor, noble or plebeian; I do not even know if the name he bears belongs to him."

"That is the only thing that chance saved him the trouble of stealing," Henryet replied. "His name is really Leone Leoni, and he belongs to one of the noblest families of Venice. His father had a small fortune and occupied the palace in which you recently lived. He had an unbounded fondness for this only son, whose precocious talents indicated a superior mental organization. Leoni was educated with care, and, when he was fifteen

years old, travelled over half of Europe with his tutor.
In five years he learned with incredible ease the language, literature and manners of the countries he visited.
His father's death brought him back to Venice with his
tutor. This tutor was Abbé Zanini, whom you must
have seen frequently at your house last winter. I do
not know whether you formed an accurate judgment of
him ; he is a man of vivid imagination, of exquisite mental keenness, of immense learning, but inconceivably im-
moral and extremely cowardly beneath a hypocritical
exterior of tolerance and sound common sense. He had
naturally depraved his pupil's conscience, and had replaced a proper understanding of justice and injustice in
his mind by an alleged knowledge of life, which consisted
in committing all the amusing escapades, all the profita-
ble sins, all the actions, good and evil, which can possibly tempt the human heart. I knew this Zanini at Paris,
and I remember hearing him say that one must know
how to do evil in order to know how to do good, and that
one must be able to find enjoyment in vice in order to be
able to find enjoyment in virtue. This man, who is
more prudent, more adroit and more cold-blooded than
Leoni, is much superior to him in knowledge ; and Leoni,
carried away by his passions or baulked by his caprices,
follows him at a distance, making innumerable false
moves which are certain to ruin him in society, and
which indeed have already ruined him, since he is at the
mercy of a few grasping confederates and a few honest
men, whose generosity he will soon tire out."

A deathlike chill froze my blood while Henryet was
speaking thus. I had to make an effort to listen to the
rest.

XVI

" At the age of twenty," continued Henryet, " Leoni found himself in possession of a reasonably handsome fortune, and entirely in control of his own movements. He was in a most advantageous position to do good; but he found his means inferior to the requirements of his ambition, and pending the time when he should build up a fortune equal to his desires, as a result of I know not what insane or culpable schemes, he squandered his inheritance in two years. His house, which he decorated with the splendor you have seen, was the rendezvous of all the dissipated youths and abandoned women of Italy. Many foreigners, connoisseurs in the matter of fast living, were received there; and thus Leoni, who had already made the acquaintance, during his travels, of many people of fashion, formed the most brilliant connections in all countries and made sure of many invaluable friends.

" As is everywhere the case, schemers and blacklegs succeeded in insinuating themselves into this large circle. I saw in Leoni's company in Paris several faces that aroused my distrust, and whose owners I suspect to-day of forming with him and the Marquis de —— an association of fashionable sharpers. Yielding to their counsels, to Zanini's lessons, or to his natural inclinations, young Leoni seems to have soon tried his hand at cheating at cards. This much is certain, that he became eminently proficient in that art and probably practised it in all the capitals of Europe without arousing the slightest suspicion. When he was absolutely ruined, he left Venice and began to travel again as an adventurer. At this point the thread of his history escapes me. Zanini, from whom I gleaned a part of what I have told you, claimed to have lost sight of him from that time and to have learned only by means of correspondence, frequently interrupted, of Leoni's innumerable changes of fortune and innumerable intrigues in society. He apologized for having produced such a pupil by saying that Leoni had perverted his doctrines; but he excused the pupil by praising the incredible cleverness, the strength of will and the presence of mind with which he had challenged fate, endured and conquered adversity. At last Leoni came to Paris with his faithful friend the Marquis de ——, whom you know, and it was there that I had an opportunity to see and judge him.

"It was Zanini who introduced him to the Princesse de X——, of whose children he was the tutor. The abbé's superior mental endowments had given him for several years past a less subordinate position in the princess's household than that usually occupied by tutors in great families. He did the honors of the salon, led the conversation, sang beautifully, and managed the concerts.

"Leoni, thanks to his wit and his talents, was welcomed with much warmth, and his company was soon sought with enthusiasm. He acquired in certain circles in Paris the same authority which you have seen him exercise over a whole provincial city. He bore himself magnificently, rarely gambled, and when he did so, always lost immense sums, which the Marquis de —— generally won. This marquis was introduced by Zanini shortly after Leoni's appearance. Although a compatriot of the latter, he pretended not to know him or rather to be prepossessed against him. He whispered in everybody's ear that they had been rivals in love at Venice,

and that, although they were both cured of their passion,
they were not cured of their hostility. Thanks to this
knavery, no one suspected them of conducting their industry in concert. They carried it on during the whole
winter without arousing the least suspicion. Sometimes
they both lost heavily, but more frequently they won,
and they lived like princes, each in his own way. One
day, a friend of mine, who had lost a large amount to
Leoni, detected an almost imperceptible signal between
him and the marquis. He said nothing, but watched
them both closely for several days. One evening, when
we had both bet on the same side, and lost as usual, he
came to me and said:

"'Look at those two Italians; I strongly suspect and
am almost certain that they cheat in concert. I have to
leave Paris on very urgent business; I leave to you the
task of following up my discovery and warning your
friends, if there is occasion to do so. You are a discreet
and prudent man ; you will not act, I hope, without being
quite sure what you are doing. In any event, if you have
trouble with the fellows, do not fail to give them my
name as the one who first accused them, and write to
me ; I will undertake to settle the dispute with one of
them.'

"He gave me his address and left Paris. I watched
the two knights of industry and acquired absolute certainty that my friend had made no mistake. I discovered
the whole secret of their knavery one evening at a party
given by the Princesse de X——. I at once took Zanini
by the arm and led him aside.

"'Are you very well acquainted,' I asked him, 'with
the two Venetians whom you introduced here?'

"'Very well,' he answered with much assurance; 'I
was the tutor of one of them and the friend of the other.'

" 'I congratulate you,' said I, 'they are a pair of black-legs.'

"I made this assertion with such confidence that he changed countenance despite his constant habit of dissimulation. I suspected him of having an interest in their winnings, and I told him that I proposed to unmask his two countrymen. He was altogether discomposed at that and earnestly entreated me not to do it. He tried to persuade me that I was mistaken. I asked him to take me to his room with the marquis. There I explained myself in a few very plain words, and the marquis, instead of denying the charge, turned pale and fainted. I do not know whether that scene was a comedy played by him and the abbé, but they appeared to me in such distress, the marquis displayed so much shame and remorse, that I was good-natured enough to allow my determination to be shaken. I demanded simply that he should leave France instantly with Leoni. The marquis promised everything; but I proposed to signify my decision to his accomplice in person, and told him to send for him. He kept us waiting a long while; at last he arrived, not humble and trembling like the other, but quivering with rage, and with clenched fists. Perhaps he expected to intimidate me by his insolence; I informed him that I was ready to give him all the satisfaction he desired, but that I should begin by accusing him publicly. At the same time I offered the marquis satisfaction on the same conditions on my friend's behalf. Leoni's impudence was disconcerted. His companions convinced him that he was lost if he resisted. He yielded, not without much remonstrance and bad temper, and they both left the house without returning to the salon. The marquis started the next day for Geneva, Leoni for Brussels.

"I was left alone with Zanini in his room; I told him

of my suspicions of him and of my purpose to denounce him to the princess. As I had no absolute proofs against him, he was less humble and suppliant than the marquis; but I saw that he was no less frightened. He exerted all the resources of his intelligence in appealing to my good nature and my discretion. I made him confess, however, that he was aware of his pupil's knavery to a certain point, and I forced him to tell me his story. In that respect, Zanini lacked prudence; he should have maintained obstinately that he knew nothing of it; but my stern threats to unmask the guests he had introduced made him lose his head. I left him, thoroughly convinced that he was a rascal, as cowardly, but more circumspect than the other two. I kept the secret in my own interest. I was afraid that the influence he had acquired over the Princesse de X—— would be stronger than my honorable character, that he would be clever enough to persuade her to regard me as an impostor or a fool, and would make my conduct appear ridiculous. I was sick of the filthy business. I thought no more about it and left Paris three months later. You know who was the first person my eyes sought as I entered Delpech's ball-room. I was still in love with you, and, having reached Brussels only an hour earlier, I did not know that you were to be married. I discovered you in the midst of the crowd; I walked toward you and saw Leoni at your side. I thought that I was dreaming, that I was deceived by a resemblance. I made inquiries and discovered beyond question that your fiancé was the knight of industry who had stolen three or four hundred louis from me. I did not hope to supplant him, indeed I think that I did not wish to. To succeed such a man in your heart, perhaps to wipe from your cheeks the marks of his kisses; that was a thought that killed my love. But I swore that an

innocent girl and an honorable family should not be the
dupes of a scoundrel. You know that our explanation
was neither long nor diffuse ; but your fatal passion de-
feated the effort that I made to save you."

Henryet paused. I hung my head, I was overwhelmed;
it seemed to me that I could never again look anybody in
the face. Henryet continued:

"Leoni avoided trouble very skilfully by carrying off
his fiancée from before my eyes, that is to say, a million
francs in diamonds which she had upon her person. He
concealed you and your jewels, I don't know where.
Amid all the tears shed over his daughter's fate, your
father shed a few for his beautiful gems so beautifully
mounted. One day he artlessly observed in my presence that the thing that grieved him most in regard to the
theft was that the diamonds would be sold for half their
value to some Jew, and that the beautiful settings, with
all their artistic workmanship, would be broken up and
melted by the receiver, to avoid compromising himself.
'It was hardly worth while to do such work!' he said,
weeping ; 'it was hardly worth while to have a daughter
and love her so dearly!'

"It would seem that your father was right, for with
the proceeds of his robbery Leoni found means to cut a
swath at Venice for only three months. The palace of his
fathers had been sold and was now to let. He hired it
and replaced his name, so they say, on the cornice of the
inner courtyard, not daring to place it over the main
gateway. As he is actually known to be a swindler by
very few people, his house became once more the rendezvous of many honorable men, who doubtless were fleeced
there by his confederates. But it may be that his fear
of being detected deterred him from joining them, for he
was speedily ruined anew. He contented himself, I pre-

sume, with winking at the brigandage those villains committed in his house; he is at their mercy and would not dare to get rid of those whom he detests most bitterly. Now he is, as you know, the Princess Zagarolo's titular lover: that lady, who has been very beautiful, is now, faded and doomed to die very soon of a disease of the lungs. It is supposed that she will leave all her property to Leoni, who pretends to be violently in love with her, and whom she loves passionately. He is waiting for her to make her will. Then you will be rich, Juliette. He has probably told you so; have patience a little longer and you will take the princess's box at the play, you will drive in her carriages, on which you will simply change the bearings; you will embrace your lover in the magnificent bed in which she will have died, you will even wear her gowns and diamonds."

It may be that the pitiless Henryet said more than this, but I heard no more; I fell to the ground in terrible convulsions.

XVII

When I came to myself, I was alone with Leoni. I was lying on a sofa. He was looking at me fondly and anxiously.

"Dear heart," he said, when he saw that I was recovering the use of my faculties, "tell me what has happened! Why did I find you in such a terrible condition? Where are you in pain? What new grief have you had?"

19

"None," I replied, and I spoke the truth, for at that moment I remembered nothing.

"You are deceiving me, Juliette; some one has distressed you. The servant who was with you when I came home told me that a man came to see you this morning, that he remained with you a long while, and that when he went out he told them to come and look after you. Who was this man, Juliette?"

I had never lied in my life; it was impossible for me to reply. I did not wish to mention Henryet's name. Leoni frowned.

"A mystery!" he said; "a mystery between us! I would never have believed you capable of it. But you know no one here! Can it be that—? If it were he, there is not blood enough in his veins to wash away his insolence! Tell me the truth, Juliette, has Chalm been here to see you? Has he persecuted you again with his vile proposals and his calumnies against me?"

"Chalm!" I exclaimed. "Is he in Milan?" And I felt a thrill of terror which must have been reflected on my face, for Leoni saw that I was ignorant of the viscount's arrival.

"If it was not he," he said to himself, "who can this caller have been, who was closeted three hours with my wife and left her in a swoon? The marquis has been with me all day."

"O heaven!" I cried, "are all your detestable associates here? In heaven's name, see that they do not find out where I live and that I do not see them."

"But who is the man you do see, and to whom you do not deny admission to your bedroom?" said Leoni, becoming more and more thoughtful and pale. "Answer me, Juliette; I insist upon it. Do you hear?"

I realized how horrible my position was becoming. I

clasped my hands, trembling, and appealed to heaven in silence.

"You do not answer," said Leoni. "Poor woman! you have little presence of mind. You have a lover, Juliette! You are not to be blamed for it, as I have a mistress. I am a fool not to be able to bear it when you are satisfied with a part of my heart and my bed. But it is certain that I cannot be so generous."

He took his hat and put on his gloves with convulsive coldness, took out his purse, placed it on the mantel, and, without another word to me—without glancing at me—left the room. I heard him walk away with an even step and descend the stairs slowly.

Surprise, dismay and fear had frozen my blood. I thought that I was going mad; I put my handkerchief in my mouth to stifle my shrieks, and then, succumbing to fatigue, fell back upon the bed in the stupor of utter prostration.

In the middle of the night I heard sounds in the room. I opened my eyes and saw, without understanding what I saw, Leoni pacing the floor in intense agitation, and the marquis seated at a table, emptying a bottle of brandy. I did not stir. I had no thought of trying to find out what they were doing there; but little by little their words, falling upon my ears, found their way to my understanding and assumed a meaning.

"I tell you that I saw him, and I am sure of it," said the marquis. "He is here."

"The infernal hound!" replied Leoni, stamping on the floor. "Would to God the earth would open and rid me of him."

"Well said!" rejoined the marquis. "That's my idea."

"He comes to my very room to torment that unfortunate woman!"

"Are you sure, Leoni, that she is not glad to have him come?"

"Hold your tongue, viper! and don't try to make me suspect that poor creature. She has nothing left in the world but my esteem."

"And Monsieur Henryet's love," added the marquis.

Leoni clenched his fists. "We will rid her of that love!" he cried, "and cure the Fleming of it."

"The devil! Leoni, don't do anything foolish!"

"And you, Lorenzo, don't you do anything vile!"

"You would call that vile, would you? We have very different ideas. You escort La Zagarolo quietly to the grave, in order to inherit her worldly goods, and you do not approve of my putting an enemy underground whose existence paralyzes ours forever! It seems to you very innocent, notwithstanding the prohibition of the physicians, to hasten by your generous fondness the end of your dear consumptive's sufferings——"

"Go to the devil! If that madwoman wants to live fast and die soon, why should I prevent her? She is attractive enough to command my obedience, and I am not fond enough of her to resist her."

"What a ghastly thing!" I muttered in spite of myself, and fell back on my pillow.

"Your wife spoke, I think," said the marquis.

"She is dreaming," Leoni replied; "she has the fever."

"Are you sure that she isn't listening?"

"In the first place she would need to have strength to listen. She is very sick, too, poor Juliette! She doesn't complain; she suffers all by herself! She has not twenty women to wait on her; she doesn't pay courtiers to satisfy her sickly fancies; she is dying piously and chastely, like an expiatory victim, between heaven and me."

Leoni sat down at the table and burst into tears.

"This is the effect of brandy," said the marquis, calmly, putting the glass to his lips. "I warned you; it always takes hold of the nerves."

"Let me alone, brute beast!" shouted Leoni, giving the table a push which nearly overturned it on the marquis; "let me weep in peace. You don't know what love is!"

"Love!" said the marquis in a theatrical tone, mimicking Leoni; "remorse! those are very sonorous and dramatic words. When do you send Juliette to the hospital?"

"That is right," said Leoni, with a gloomy, despairing air, "talk to me that way, I prefer it. That suits me, I am capable of anything. To the hospital! yes. She was so lovely, so dazzlingly beautiful! I came, and see what I have brought her to! Ah! I could tear out my hair!"

"Well," said the marquis after a pause, "have we had enough sentiment for to-day? God! it has been a long attack. Now let us reason a little; you don't seriously mean to fight with Henryet?"

"Most seriously," replied Leoni; "you talk seriously enough about murdering him."

"That's a very different matter."

"It is precisely the same thing. He doesn't know how to use any weapon, and I am very expert with all sorts."

"Except the stiletto," said the marquis, "or the pistol at point-blank range; besides, you don't kill anybody but women."

"I will kill that man at all events," replied Leoni.

"And you think he will consent to fight with you?"

"He will; he is brave enough."

"But he isn't mad. He will begin by having us arrested as a couple of thieves."

"He will begin by giving me satisfaction. I will force him to do it, I will strike him in the theatre."

"He will return it by calling you forger, blackleg, card-sharper."

"He will have to prove it. He is not known here, whereas we are fairly established here on a brilliant footing. I will call him a lunatic and visionary; and when I have killed him, everybody will think I was right."

"You are mad, my dear fellow," replied the marquis; "Henryet is recommended to the richest merchants in Italy. His family is well known and bears a high reputation in commercial circles. He himself doubtless has friends in the city, or at all events acquaintances, with whom his statements will carry weight. He will fight to-morrow night, let us say. Very good! during the day he will have had time enough to tell twenty people that he is going to fight with you because he caught you cheating, and that you took it ill of him that he should try to prevent you."

"Very well! he may say it and people may believe it if they choose, but I will kill him."

"La Zagarolo will turn you out-of-doors and destroy her will. All the nobles will close their doors to you, and the police will request you to go to play the lover in some other country."

"Very well! I will go somewhere else. The rest of the world will belong to me when I am well rid of that man."

"Yes, and from his blood will sprout a pretty little nursery of accusers. Instead of Monsieur Henryet, you will have the whole city of Milan at your heels."

"O heaven! what shall I do?" said Leoni, in sore perplexity.

" Make an appointment with him in your wife's name, and cool his blood with a good hunting-knife. Give me that scrap of paper yonder and I'll write to him."

Leoni, paying no heed, opened a window and fell into a reverie, while the marquis wrote. When he had finished he called him.

" Listen to this, Leoni," he said, "and see whether I know how to write a *billet-doux*:

" 'My friend; I cannot receive you again in my room; Leoni knows all and threatens me with the most horrible consequences; take me away or I am lost. Take me to my mother or put me in a convent; do with me as you please, but rescue me from my present horrible plight. Be in front of the main door of the cathedral at one o'clock to-morrow morning, and we will make arrangements for our departure. It will be easy for me to meet you, as Leoni passes every night at La Zagarolo's. Do not be surprised by this extraordinary and almost illegible handwriting: Leoni, in a fit of anger, almost crushed my right hand.

" 'JULIETTE RUYTER.'

" It seems to me that that letter is very judiciously expressed," said the marquis, "and that it will seem plausible enough to the Fleming, whatever the degree of intimacy between him and your wife. The words which she fancied that she was saying to him at times in her delirium make it certain that he offered to take her back to her own country. The writing is horrible, and whether he is familiar with Juliette's or not——"

" Let me see it," said Leoni, leaning over the table with an air of interest.

His face wore a horrifying expression of doubt and longing to be persuaded. I saw no more. My brain was exhausted, my thoughts became confused. I relapsed into a sort of lethargy.

XVIII

When I came to myself the flickering lamplight fell upon the same objects. I raised myself cautiously and saw the marquis just where he was when I lost consciousness. It was still dark. There were still bottles on the table, as well as a writing-desk and something which I could not see very plainly, but which resembled a weapon. Leoni was standing in the middle of the room. I tried to recall their previous conversation. I hoped that the ghastly fragments of it which recurred to my memory were merely the dreams of fever, and I had no idea at first that twenty-four hours had elapsed between that conversation and the one just beginning. The first words that I understood were these :

" He must have suspected something for he was armed to the teeth."

As he spoke, Leoni wiped his bleeding hand with his handkerchief.

"Bah! yours is nothing but a scratch," said the marquis; "I have a more severe wound in the leg; and yet I must dance at the ball to-morrow, so that no one may suspect anything. So stop fussing over your hand, wrap it up and think of something else."

" It is impossible for me to think of anything but that

blood. It seems to me that
me."

"Your nerves are too del
for nothing."

"*Canaille!*" exclaimed L
and contempt, "but for m
man; you retreated like a cc
been struck from behind. I
were lost, and if your ruin

mine, I would never have touched that man at such
an hour and in such a place. But your infernal obstinacy compelled me to be your accomplice. All that
I needed was to commit a murder, to be worthy of your
society."

"Don't play the modest man," retorted the marquis;
"when you saw that he defended himself, you became a
very tiger."

"Ah! yes, it rejoiced my heart to have him die defend-
ing himself; for after all I killed him fairly."

"Very fairly; he had postponed the game till the next
day, and as you were in a hurry to be done with it, you
killed him on the spot."

"Whose fault was it, traitor? Why did you throw
yourself on him just as we were separating after we had
agreed to meet the next day? Why did you run when
you saw that he was armed, and thus compel me to
defend you or else be denounced by him to-morrow for
having conspired with you to lure him into a trap and
murder him? Now I have made myself liable to the
scaffold, and yet I am not a murderer. I fought with
equal weapons, equal chance, equal courage."

"Yes, he defended himself like a man," said the marquis; "you both performed prodigies of valor. It was a
very fine spectacle to see, truly Homeric, was that duel

ves. But I am bound to say that for a Venetian
andle that weapon wretchedly."

It is quite true that it isn't the weapon I am in the
habit of using, and by the way I am inclined to think
it would be wise to conceal or destroy this one."

"That would be the height of folly, my friend! You
must keep it; your servants and friends know that you
always carry such a weapon; if you should dispose of it,
that would be an indication of guilt."

"True, but yours?"

"Mine is innocent of his blood; my first blows missed,
and after that yours left me no room."

"Ah! heaven! that is true too. You tried to murder
him, and fatality compelled me to do with my own hands
the deed of which I had such a horror."

"It pleases you to say that, my dear fellow; however,
you went very willingly to the rendezvous."

"I had an instinctive foreboding that my evil genius
would force me to do it. After all, it was my destiny
and his. We are rid of him at last! But why in the
devil did you empty his pockets?"

"Precaution and presence of mind on my part. When
they find him stripped of his money and his wallet, they
will look for the assassin among the lowest classes, and
will never suspect people in fashionable society. It will
be considered an act of brigandage and not a matter of
private revenge. Don't betray yourself by absurd emotion when you hear the affair mentioned to-morrow, and
we have nothing to fear. Just reach me the candle so
that I can burn these papers; as for honest coin, that
never betrayed anybody."

"Stop!" said Leoni, seizing a letter which the marquis
was about to burn with the rest. "I saw Juliette's family
name."

"It is a letter to Madame Ruyter," said the marquis.
"Let us see :"

"'MADAME,

"'If it is not too late, if you did not start at once on
receiving the letter I wrote yesterday summoning you to
your daughter, do not start. Wait at home for her or
come to meet her as far as Strasbourg; I will send for you
when we reach there. I shall be there with Mademoiselle
Ruyter in a few days. She has decided to fly from her
seducer's dishonor and ill treatment. I have just received
a note in which she announces this determination. I am
to see her to-night to agree upon the time of our departure. I will leave all my business in order to make the
most of her present disposition, in which her lover's flat-
teries may not leave her forever. The empire that he
has over her is still immense. I fear that her passion for
that wretch is eternal, and that her regret for having left
him will make you both shed many tears hereafter. Be
indulgent and kind to her; that is your proper rôle as her
mother, and you can easily play it. For my part, I am
rough-mannered, and my indignation finds expression
more readily than my compassion. I wish I were more
persuasive; but I cannot be more lovable, and it is my
destiny not to be loved.

"'PAUL HENRYET.'

"This proves to you, O my friend!" said the marquis
in a mocking tone, as he held the letter in the flame of
the candle, "that your wife is faithful and that you are
the most fortunate of husbands."

"Poor woman!" said Leoni, "and poor Henryet! He
would have made her happy! He would at least have
respected and honored her! In God's name, what fatal-

ity drove her into the arms of a wretched adventurer, drawn to her by destiny from one end of the world to the other, when she had an honorable man's heart at her very hand. Blind child! why did you choose me?"

"Charming!" said the marquis ironically. "I hope you will write some verses on this subject. A pretty epitaph for the man you massacred to-night would be, to my mind, in exceedingly good taste and altogether new."

"Yes, I will write one for him," retorted Leoni, "and it will run like this:

"'Here lies an honest man who tried to defend human justice against two scoundrels, and whom divine justice allowed them to murder.'"

Thereupon, Leoni fell into a sorrowful reverie, during which he constantly muttered his victim's name:

"Paul Henryet!" he said. "Twenty-two years old, twenty-four at most. A cold but handsome face. A rigid, upright character. Hatred of injustice. The uncompromising pride of honesty, and withal something tender and melancholy. He loved Juliette, he has always loved her. He fought against his passion to no purpose. I see by that letter that he loved her still, and that he would have worshipped her if he could have cured her. Juliette, Juliette! you might still have been happy with him, and I have killed him! I have robbed you of the man who might have comforted you; your only defender is no more, and you remain the victim of a bandit."

"Very fine!" said the marquis; "I wish that you might never move your lips without having a stenographer beside you to preserve all the noble and affecting things you say. For my part, I am going to bed. Good-night, my dear fellow; go to bed to your wife, but change your shirt first; for, deuce take me! you have Henryet's blood on your frill!"

The marquis left the room. Leoni, after a moment's irresolution, came to my bed, raised the curtain and looked at me. He saw that I was only drowsing under my bedclothes, and that my eyes were open and fixed upon him. He could not endure my livid face and fixed stare; he fell back with a cry of horror, and I called him several times in a weak, broken voice: "Murderer! murderer! murderer!"

He fell on his knees as if struck by lightning, and dragged himself to my bed with an imploring air.

"Go to bed to your wife," I said, repeating the marquis's words in a sort of delirium; "but change your shirt, for you have Henryet's blood on your frill!"

Leoni fell face downward on the floor, uttering inarticulate cries. I lost my reason altogether, and it seemed to me that I repeated his cries, imitating with dazed servility the tone of his voice and the contortions of his body. He thought that I was mad, and, springing to his feet in terror, came to my side. I thought that he was going to kill me; I threw myself out of bed, crying: "Mercy! mercy! I won't tell!" and I fainted just as he seized me, to lift me up and assist me.

XIX

I awoke, still in his arms, and he had never put forth so much eloquence, so much affection, so many tears, to implore his pardon. He confessed that he was the lowest of men; but, he said, there was one thing, and only one, that raised him somewhat in his eyes, and that was

the love he had always had for me, and which none of
his vices, none of his crimes had had the power to stifle.
Hitherto he had fought against the appearances which
accused him on all sides. He had struggled against over-
whelming evidence in order to retain my esteem. Thenceforth, being no longer able to justify himself by false-
hood, he took a different course and assumed a new rôle,
in order to move me and conquer me. He laid aside all
artifice—perhaps I should say all sense of shame—and
confessed all the villainy of his life. But amid all that
filth he forced me to distinguish and to understand what
there was in his character that was truly noble, the faculty of loving, the everlasting vigor of a heart in which
the most exhausting weariness, the most dangerous
trials, did not extinguish the sacred flame.

"My conduct is base," he said to me, "but my heart
is still noble. It still bleeds for its crimes ; it has retained, in all the vigor of its first youth, the sentiment
of justice and injustice, horror of the evil it does, enthusiastic admiration of the good it beholds. Your patience,
your virtues, your angelic kindliness, your pity, as inexhaustible as God's, can never be displayed in favor of a
being who appreciates them better or admires them more.
A man of regular morals and sensitive conscience would
consider them more natural and would appreciate them
less. With such a man you would be simply a virtuous
woman ; while with a man like me you are a sublime
woman, and the debt of gratitude which is piling up in
my heart is as great as your sacrifices and your sufferings. Ah ! it is something to be loved and to be entitled
to a boundless passion, and from what other man have
you so good a right to claim such a passion as from me ?
For whom would you subject yourself again to the tortures and the despair you have undergone ? Do you

think there is anything else in life but love? For my
part, I do not. And do you think that it is a simple matter
to inspire it and to feel it? Thousands of men die incomplete, having never known any other love than that
of the beasts. Often a heart capable of loving seeks in
vain where to bestow its love, and comes forth pure of all
earthly passions, perhaps to find a place in heaven. Ah!
when God vouchsafes to us on earth that profound, passionate, ineffable sentiment, we must no longer desire or
hope for paradise, Juliette; for paradise is the blending
of two hearts in a kiss of love. And when we have
found it here on earth, what matters it whether it be in
the arms of a saint or of one of the damned? What matters it whether the man you love be accursed or adored
among men, so long as he returns your love? Is it I
whom you love, or is it this noise that is going on about
me? What did you love in me at the outset? Was it
the splendor that encompassed me? If you hate me to-
day, I must needs doubt your past love; I must needs
see in you, instead of that angel, that devoted victim
whose blood, shed for me, falls ceaselessly drop by drop
upon my lips, only a poor, weak, credulous girl, who
loved me from vanity and deserted me from selfishness.
Juliette, Juliette, think of what you will do if you leave
me! You will ruin the only friend who knows you, appreciates and respects you, for a society which despises
you now and whose esteem you will never recover.
You have nothing left but me in the whole world, my
poor child. You must either cling to the adventurer's
fortunes or die forgotten in a convent. If you leave me,
you are no less insane than cruel; you will have had all
your misery, all your sufferings, and you will not reap
their fruit; for now, if, notwithstanding all that you
know, you can still love me and stay with me, be sure

that I will love you with a love of which you have no conception, and which I never should have dreamed of as possible if I had married you honestly and lived with you peacefully in the bosom of your family. Hitherto, despite all you have sacrificed, all you have suffered, I have not loved you as I feel that I am capable of loving. You have never yet loved me as I am ; you have cherished an attachment for a false Leoni, in whom you still saw some grandeur and some fascination. You hoped that he would become some day the man you loved in the beginning ; you did not believe that you had held in your arms a man who was irrevocably lost. And I said to myself : ' She loves me conditionally ; it is not I whom she loves as yet, but the character I am acting. When she sees my features under my mask, she will cover her eyes and fly; she will look with horror on the lover whom now she presses to her bosom. No, she is not the wife and mistress I had dreamed of, and for whom my ardent heart is calling with all its strength. Juliette is still a part of that society whose foe I am ; she will be my foe when she knows me. I cannot confide in her ; I cannot pour out upon the bosom of any living being the most execrable of my sufferings, my shame for what I am doing every day. I suffer, I am heaping up remorse in my soul. If only there were a woman capable of loving me without asking me to change—if I could have a friend who would not be an accuser and a judge ! '— That is what I thought, Juliette. I prayed to heaven for that friend, but I prayed that it might be you and no other ; for you were already what I loved best on earth before. I realized all that there still remained for us both to do before loving each other really.''

What could I reply to such speeches ? I looked at him with a stupefied air. I was amazed that I still considered

him handsome and lovable ; that I still felt in his presence the same emotion, the same desire for his caresses,
the same gratitude for his love. His degradation left no
trace on his noble brow; and when his great black eyes
flashed their flame upon mine, I was dazzled, intoxicated
as always ; all his blemishes disappeared, everything was
blotted out, even the stains of Henryet's blood. I forgot
everything else to bind myself to him by blind vows, by
oaths and insane embraces. Then in very truth his love
was rekindled or rather renewed, as he had prophesied.
He gradually abandoned the Princess Zagarolo and passed
all the time of my convalescence at my feet, with the
same loving attentions and the delicate tokens of affection
which had made me so happy in Switzerland ; I can say,
indeed, that these proofs of affection were even more ardent and caused me more pride, that that was the happi-
est period of my whole life, and that Leoni was never
dearer to me. I was convinced of the truth of all that he
had told me; nor could I fear that he clung to me from
self-interest, as I had nothing more in the world to give
him, and was thenceforth a burden to him and dependent
upon the hazards of his fortunes. However I felt a sort
of pride in not falling short of what he expected from my
generosity, and his gratitude seemed to me greater than
my sacrifices.

One evening he came home in a state of great excitement, and said, pressing me to his heart again and again :

" My Juliette, my sister, my wife, my angel, you must
be as kind and indulgent as God himself, you must give
me a fresh proof of your adorable sweetness and your
heroism ; you must come and live with me at the Princess Zagarolo's."

I recoiled, surprised beyond words; and, as I realized
that it was no longer in my power to deny him anything,

20

I turned pale and began to tremble like a condemned man at the gallows' foot.

"Listen," he said, "the princess is horribly ill. I have neglected her on your account; she has grieved so that her disease has become seriously aggravated and the doctors give her only a month to live. Since you know everything, I can speak to you about that infernal will. It is a matter of several millions, and I am in competition with a family on the alert to take advantage of my mistakes and turn me out at the decisive moment. The will in my favor is in existence, in proper form, but a moment's anger may destroy it. We are ruined, we have no other resource. You will have to go to the hospital and I become a leader of brigands, if it escapes us."

"O *mon Dieu!*" I said, "we lived so inexpensively in Switzerland! Why is wealth a necessity to us? Now that we love each other so well, can we not live happily without committing any new villainy?"

He answered by a frown which expressed the disappointment, the annoyance and the dread which my reproaches caused him. I said nothing more in that connection, but asked him wherein I was necessary to the success of his enterprise.

"Because the princess, in a fit of jealousy not without some foundation, has demanded to see you and question you. My enemies have taken pains to inform her that I pass all my mornings with a young and pretty woman who came to Milan after me. For a long time I succeeded in making her believe that you were my sister; but, during this month that I have neglected her altogether, she has conceived doubts, and refuses to believe in your illness, which I alleged as an excuse for my neglect.—'If your sister is sick too, and can't do without you,' she said, 'have her brought to my house; my women and my doctors will take care of her. You can see her at any time; and if she is really your sister, I will love her as if she were my sister too.'—I tried in vain to fight against this strange whim. I told her that you were very poor and very proud, that nothing in the world would induce you to accept her hospitality, and that it would, in fact, be exceedingly unseemly and indelicate for you to come to live in the house of your brother's mistress. She would listen to no excuse and replied to all my objections with: 'I see that you are deceiving me; she is not your sister.'—If you refuse, we are lost. Come, come, come; I implore you, my child, come!"

I took my hat and shawl without replying. While I was dressing, tears rolled slowly down my cheeks. As we left my chamber, Leoni wiped them away with his lips and embraced me again and again, calling me his benefactress, his guardian angel and his only friend.

I passed with trembling limbs through the princess's vast apartments. When I saw the magnificence of the house, I had an indescribable feeling of oppression at my heart, and I remembered Henryet's harsh words: "When she is dead, you will be rich, Juliette; you will inherit her splendor, you will sleep in her bed and you can wear her gowns."—I hung my head as I passed the servants; it seemed to me that they glared at me with hatred and envy; and I felt far beneath them. Leoni pressed my arm in his, feeling my body tremble and my legs give way.

"Courage! courage!" he whispered to me.

We reached the bedroom at last. The princess was lying in an invalid's chair and seemed to be awaiting us impatiently. She was a woman of about thirty years, very thin, with a yellow face, and magnificently dressed, although *en déshabillé*. She must have been very beau-

tiful in her early days, and she still had a charming face.
The thinness of her cheeks exaggerated the size of her
eyes, the whites of which, vitrified by consumption, resembled mother of pearl. Her fine, smooth hair was of
a glistening black and seemed dry and sickly like her
whole person. When she saw me, she uttered a faint
exclamation of joy and held out a long, tapering hand, of
a bluish tinge, which I fancy that I can see at this moment. I understood, by a glance from Leoni, that I was
expected to kiss that hand, and I resigned myself to the
necessity.

Leoni was undoubtedly ill at ease, and yet his self-
possession and the tranquillity of his manners confounded
me. He spoke of me to his mistress as if there were no
possibility of her discovering his knavery, and expressed
his affection for her before me, as if it were impossible for
me to feel any grief or anger. The princess seemed to
have fits of distrust from time to time, and I could see, by
her glances and her words, that she was studying me in
order to destroy her suspicions or confirm them. As my
natural mildness of disposition made it impossible for her
to hate me, she soon began to have confidence in me ;
and, jealous as she was, to the point of frenzy, she
thought that it was impossible for any woman to consent
to take the part I was playing. An adventuress might
have done it, but my manners and my face gave the lie
to any such conjecture as to my character. The princess
became passionately fond of me. She would hardly
allow me to leave her bedroom, she overwhelmed me
with gifts and caresses. I was a little humiliated by her
generosity and I longed to refuse her gifts ; but the fear
of displeasing Leoni made me endure this additional mor-
tification. What I had to suffer during the first days,
and the efforts that I made to bend my pride to that ex-

tent, are beyond belief. However, the suffering gradually became less keen, and my mental plight became en-
durable. Leoni manifested in secret a passionate gratitude and delirious fondness. The princess, despite her
whims, her impatience, and all the torture that her love
for Leoni caused me, became agreeable and almost dear
to me. Her heart was ardent rather than loving, and her
nature lavish rather than generous. But she had an irresistible charm of manner; the wit with which her language
sparkled in the midst of her most intense agony, the in-
geniously kind and caressing words with which she
thanked me for my attentions or begged me to forget her
outbreaks of temper, her little cajoleries, her shrewd ob-
servations, the coquetry which attended her to the grave;
in short, everything about her had an originality, a
nobility, a refinement by which I was the more deeply
impressed because I had never seen a woman of her rank
at close quarters, and was not accustomed to the great
charm which they owe to their familiarity with the best
society. She possessed that charm to such a degree that
I could not resist it and allowed myself to be swayed by
it at her pleasure; she was so coy and fascinating with
Leoni that I imagined that he was really in love with her,
and ended by becoming accustomed to see them kiss, and
to listen to their insipid speeches without being revolted
by them. Indeed, there were days when they were so
charming and so witty that I really enjoyed listening to
them; and Leoni found means to say such sweet things
to me that I was happy even in my unspeakable degradation.

The ill-will which the servants and underlings displayed toward me at first was speedily allayed, thanks to
the pains I took to turn over to them all the little gifts
their mistress gave me. I even enjoyed the affection and

confidence of the nephews and cousins; a very pretty little niece, whom the princess obstinately refused to see, was smuggled into her presence by my assistance, and pleased her exceedingly. Thereupon, I begged her to allow me to give the child a pretty casket which she had forced upon me that morning; and this display of generosity led her to give the child a much more valuable present. Leoni, in whose greed there was nothing paltry or petty, was pleased to see this bounty bestowed on a poor orphan, and the other relations began to believe that they had nothing to fear from us, and that our friendship for the princess was purely noble and disinterested. The essays at tale-bearing against me ceased entirely, and for two months we led a very tranquil life. I was astonished to find that I was almost happy.

XX

The only thing that disturbed me seriously was the constant presence of the Marquis de ——. He had obtained an introduction to the princess, on what pretext I have no idea, and amused her by his caustic, ill-natured chatter. Then he would draw Leoni into another room and have long interviews with him, from which Leoni always came with a gloomy brow.

"I hate and despise Lorenzo," he often said to me; "he is the vilest cur I know; he is capable of anything."

Thereupon, I would urge him to break with him; but he always replied:

"It is impossible, Juliette; don't you know that when two rascals have acted together, they never fall out except to send each other to the scaffold?"

These ominous words sounded so strangely in that beautiful palace, amid the peaceful life we were leading, and almost within hearing of that gracious and trustful princess, that a shudder ran through my veins when I heard them.

Meanwhile, our dear invalid's suffering increased from day to day, and the moment soon came when she must inevitably give up the struggle. We saw that she was failing gradually; but she did not lose her presence of mind for an instant, nor cease her jests and her kind speeches.

"How sorry I am," she said to Leoni, "that Juliette is your sister! Now that I am going to the other world, I must renounce you. I can neither demand nor desire that you remain faithful to me after my death. Unfortunately, you are certain to make a fool of yourself and throw yourself at the head of some woman who is unworthy of you. I know nobody in the world but your sister who is good enough for you; she is an angel, and no one but you is worthy of her."

I could not resist this kindly flattery, and my affection for the princess became warmer and warmer as death slowly took her from us. I could not believe it possible that she would be taken away with all her faculties, all her tranquillity, and when we were all so happy together. I asked myself how we could possibly live without her, and I could not think of her great gilded armchair standing unoccupied, between Leoni and myself, without my eyes filling with tears.

One evening, when I was reading to her while Leoni sat on the carpet warming her feet in a muff, she re-

ceived a letter, read it through hastily, uttered a loud
shriek and fainted. While I flew to her assistance, Leoni
picked up the letter and ran his eye over it. Although
the writing was disguised, he recognized the hand of the
Vicomte de Chalm. It was a denunciation of me, with
circumstantial details concerning my family, my abduction, my relations with Leoni; and, with all the rest, a
mass of detestable falsehoods regarding my morals and
my character.

At the shriek which the princess uttered, Lorenzo,
who was always hovering about us like a bird of evil
omen, entered the room, I know not how; and Leoni,
taking him into a corner, showed him the viscount's
letter. When they came back to us, the marquis was
very calm, and had a mocking smile on his lips, as usual;
while Leoni, intensely agitated, seemed to question him
with his eyes as if to ask his advice.

The princess was still unconscious in my arms. The
marquis shrugged his shoulders.

" Your wife is intolerably stupid," he said, so loud that
I overheard him. " Her presence here now will have
the worst possible effect. Send her away; tell her to go
for help. I will take everything on myself."

" But what will you do ? " said Leoni, in great anxiety.

" Never fear. I have had an expedient all ready for
a long while; it's a paper that I always have about me.
But send Juliette away."

Leoni asked me to call the servants. I obeyed, and
laid the princess's head gently on a cushion. But just as
I was passing through the door, some undefinable magnetic force stopped me and made me turn. I saw the
marquis approach the invalid as if to assist her; but his
face seemed so wicked and Leoni's so pale, that I was
afraid to leave the dying woman alone with them.

Heaven knows what vague ideas passed through my brain. I hastened to the bed and, glancing at Leoni in terror, I said: "Beware! beware!"—"Of what?" he replied, with an air of amazement. In truth I did not know myself, and I was ashamed of the species of madness I had shown. The marquis's ironical air completed my discomfiture. I went out and returned a moment later with the princess's women and the physician. He found the princess suffering from a terrible nervous spasm, and said that we must try to make her swallow a spoonful of her sedative mixture at once. We tried in vain to force her teeth apart.

"Let the signora try it," said one of the women, pointing to me; "the princess won't take anything from anybody else, and never refuses what she gives her."

I did try, and the dying woman readily yielded. Through force of habit she pressed my hand feebly as she returned the spoon to me; then she violently threw up her arms, raised herself as if she were about to jump out of bed, and fell back dead on her pillow.

This sudden death made a terrible impression on me; I fainted and was carried from the room. I was ill several days, and, when I returned to life, Leoni informed me that I was thenceforth in my own house; that the will had been opened and found unassailable in every respect; that we were the possessors of a handsome fortune and a magnificent palace.

"I owe it all to you, Juliette," he said, "and, more than that, I owe it to you that I am able to think without shame or remorse of our friend's last moments. Your delicacy, your angelic goodness, encompassed them with attentions and lessened their melancholy. She died in your arms, that rival whom any other woman than you would have strangled; and you wept for her as if she were your sister! You are good! too good, too good! Now enjoy the fruit of your courage ; see how happy I am to be rich and to be able to surround you once more with all the luxury that you crave."

"Hush," I replied; "now is the time when I blush and suffer. So long as that woman was here, and I was sacrificing my love and my pride to her, I took comfort in the thought that I was really fond of her, and that I was sacrificing myself for her and for you. Now I see only what was base and detestable in my situation. How everybody must despise us!"

"You are greatly mistaken, my dear girl," said Leoni ; "everybody bows down to us and honors us because we are rich."

But Leoni did not long enjoy his triumph. The heirs-at-law, who came from Rome furious against us, having learned the details of the princess's sudden demise, accused us of having hastened it by poison, and demanded that the body should be exhumed to ascertain the facts. That was done, and, at the first glance, the traces of a powerful poison were discovered.

"We are lost!" said Leoni, rushing into my room. "Ildegonda was poisoned, and we are accused of having done it. Who could have committed that abominable crime? We must not ask the question, for it was Satan with Lorenzo's face. That is how he serves us. He is safe, and we are in the hands of the law. Do you feel the courage to leap out of the window?"

"No," I said; "I am innocent; I fear nothing. If you are guilty, fly."

"I am not guilty, Juliette," he said, squeezing my arm fiercely. "Do not accuse me when I do not accuse myself. You know that I am not in the habit of sparing myself."

We were arrested and thrown into prison. The prose-
cution made much noise, but it was less protracted and
its result less serious than people expected. Our inno-
cence saved us. In face of such a horrible charge I recovered all the strength due to a pure conscience. My
youth and my air of sincerity won the judges at the very
beginning. I was speedily acquitted. Leoni's honor and
life hung in the balance a little longer. But it was impossible, despite appearances, to find any proof against
him, for he was not guilty. He was horror-stricken by
the crime—his face and his answers said so plainly
enough. He came forth purged of that accusation. All
the servants were suspected. The marquis had disappeared, but he returned secretly the moment that we
were discharged from prison, and presumed to order Leoni
to divide the inheritance with him. He declared that we
owed him everything ; that, except for the audacity and
prompt execution of his plan, the will would have been
destroyed. Leoni made the most terrific threats, but the
marquis was not frightened. He had the murder of Henryet as a weapon to hold Leoni in awe, and he had it in
his power to ruin him utterly. Leoni, frantic with rage,
resigned himself to the necessity of paying him a considerable sum.

 We began at once to lead a life of wild dissipation and
to display the most immeasurable magnificence : to ruin
himself anew was with Leoni a matter of six short months.
I saw without regret the disappearance of the wealth
which I had acquired with shame and sorrow ; but I was
terrified for Leoni's sake at the near approach of poverty.
I knew that he could not endure it, and that to escape
from it, he would plunge into fresh misconduct and fresh
dangers. Unfortunately it was impossible to induce him
to practise self-restraint and prudence; he replied with

caresses or jests to my entreaties and warnings. He had fifteen English horses in his stable, his table was open to the whole city, and he had a troupe of musicians at his orders. But the principal cause of his ruin was the enormous sums he was compelled to give his former associates, to prevent them from swooping down upon him and making his house a den of thieves. He had induced them to agree not to ply their trade under his roof; and, to persuade them to leave the salon when his guests began to play cards, he was obliged to pay them a considerable sum every day. This intolerable servitude made him long sometimes to fly from the world and conceal himself with me in some peaceful retreat. But truth compels me to say that that prospect was even more appalling to him; for the affection he felt for me was not strong enough to fill his whole life. He was always kind to me, but, as at Venice, he neglected me to drink his fill of all the pleasures of wealth. He led the most dissolute life away from home, and kept several mistresses, whom he selected from a certain fashionable set, to whom he made magnificent presents, and whose society flattered his insatiable vanity. Base and sordid in the acquisition of wealth, he was superb in his prodigality. His fickle character changed with his fortune, and his love for me followed all its phases. In the agitation and suffering caused by his reverses, having nobody but me in all the world to pity him and love him, he returned to me with heartfelt joy; but in his pleasures he forgot me and sought keener delights elsewhere. I was aware of all his infidelities; whether from indolence, or indifference, or confidence in my unwearying forgiveness, he no longer took the trouble to conceal them from me; and when I reproved him for the indelicacy of such frankness, he reminded me of my conduct toward the Princess Zagarolo,

and asked me if my pity were already exhausted. Thus
the past bound me irrevocably to patience and grief. The
greatest injustice in Leoni's conduct was his apparent belief that I was ready to submit to all these sacrifices thenceforth, without pain, and that a woman could ever become
accustomed to overcome her jealousy.

I received a letter from my mother, who had heard of
me at last through Henryet, and who had fallen danger-
ously ill just as she was starting to join me. She implored me to go to take care of her, and promised to
welcome me with gratitude and without reproaches.
That letter was a thousand times too gentle and too kind.
I bathed it with my tears; but, argue with myself as I
would, it seemed to me not what it should be; it was so
mild and humble in tone and expression as to be undig-
nified. Must I say it?—it was not the pardon of a noble
and loving mother, alas! but the appeal of a sick and
bored woman. I started at once and found her dying.
She blessed me, pardoned me and died in my arms, re-
questing me to see that she was buried in a certain dress
of which she had been very fond.

XXI

So much fatigue of body and mind, so much suffering
had almost exhausted my sensibility. I hardly wept
for my mother; I shut myself up in her room after they
had taken her body away, and there I remained, crushed
and despondent, for several months, occupied solely in
reviewing the past in all its phases, and never bethinking

myself to wonder what I should do in the future. My
aunt, who had greeted me very coldly at first, was
touched by this mute grief, which her character understood better than the more demonstrative form of tears.
She looked after my welfare in silence, and saw to it that
I did not allow myself to die of hunger. The melancholy
aspect of that house, which I had known so cheerful and
bright, was well adapted to my frame of mind. I saw
the old furniture, which recalled the numberless trivial
events of my childhood. I compared that time, when a
scratch on my finger was the most terrible catastrophe
that could disturb the tranquillity of my family, with the
infamous and blood-stained life I had subsequently led.
I saw, on the one hand, my mother at the ball, on the
other, the Princess Zagarolo dying of poison in my arms,
perhaps by my hand. The music of the violins echoed
in my dreams amid the shrieks of the murdered Henryet;
and, in the seclusion of the prison, where, during three
months of agony, I had seemed to hear a sentence of
death each day, I saw coming toward me, amid the glare
of candles and the perfume of flowers, my own ghost clad
in silver crêpe and covered with jewels. Sometimes, tired
out by these confused and terrifying dreams, I walked to
the window, raised the curtains and looked out upon that
city where I had been so happy and so flattered, and on
the trees of that promenade where so much admiration
had followed my every step. But I soon noticed the insulting curiosity which my pale face aroused. People
stopped under my window or stood in groups talking
about me, almost pointing their fingers at me. Then I
would step back, drop the curtains, sit down beside my
mother's bed and remain there until my aunt came with
her silent face and noiseless step, took my arm and led
me to the table. Her manner toward me at that crisis of

my life, seemed to me most generous and most appro-
priate to my situation. I would not have listened to words
of consolation, I could not have endured reproaches, I
should not have put faith in marks of esteem. Silent affection and unobtrusive compassion made more impression on me. That dismal face, which moved noiselessly
about me like a ghost, like a reminder of the past, was
the only face that neither disturbed nor terrified me.
Sometimes I took her dry hands and held them to my lips
for several minutes, without giving vent to a sigh. She
never replied to that caress, but stood patiently, and did
not withdraw her hands from my kisses; that was
much.

I no longer thought of Leoni except as a ghastly memory which I sought with all my strength to banish. The
thought of returning to him made me shudder as the sight
of an execution would have done. I had not energy
enough remaining to love him or hate him. He did not
write to me and I was hardly aware of it, I had counted
so little on his letters. One day there came one which
told me of new disasters. A will of the Princess Zagarolo had been found, bearing a later date than ours. One
of her servants, in whom she had confidence, had had
the will in his custody ever since the day of its date.
She had made it at the time that Leoni had neglected her
to take care of me, and she was doubtful as to our re-
lationship. Afterward, when she became reconciled to
us, she had intended to destroy it; but, as she was subject to innumerable whims, she had kept both wills, so
that she might at any time decide which she would leave
in force. Leoni knew where his was kept; but the existence of the other was known only to Vincenzo, the
princess's man of confidence; and he was under in-
structions to burn it at a sign from her. She did not an-

ticipate, poor creature, such a sudden and violent death. Vincenzo, whom Leoni had laden with benefactions, and who was altogether devoted to him at that time, having moreover no knowledge of the princess's final intentions, kept the will without saying a word, and allowed us to produce ours. He might have enriched himself by threatening us or selling his secret to the heirs-at-law ; but he was not a dishonest man nor a wicked one. He allowed us to enjoy the inheritance, demanding no higher wages than he had previously received. But, when I had left Leoni, he became dissatisfied; for Leoni was brutal with his servants, and I retained them in his service only by my indulgence. One day Leoni forgot himself so far as to strike the old man, who at once pulled the will from his pocket and told him that he was going to take it to the princess's cousins. Threats, entreaties, offers of money, all were powerless to appease his anger. The marquis appeared on the scene and attempted to obtain possession of the fatal paper by force ; but Vincenzo, who was a remarkably powerful man for his years, knocked him down, struck him, threatened to throw Leoni through the window if he attacked him, and hurried away to publish the document that avenged him. Leoni was at once dispossessed, and ordered to restore all that he had expended of the property, that is to say, three fourths of it. As he was unable to comply, he tried to fly, but in vain. He was put into prison, and it was from the prison that he wrote to me, not all the details which I have given you and which I learned afterward, but a few words in which he depicted the horror of his position. If I did not go to his aid, he might languish all his life in the most horrible captivity, for he no longer had the means to procure the comforts with which we had been able to surround ourselves at the time of our former confinement.

His friends had abandoned him and perhaps were glad to be rid of him. He was absolutely without resources, in a damp cell, where he was already very ill with fever. His jewels, even his linen had been sold; he had almost nothing to protect him from the cold.

I started at once. As I had never intended to settle definitively in Brussels, and as naught but the indolence of grief had delayed me there for half a year, I had converted almost all of my inheritance into cash; I had often thought of using it to found a hospital for penitent girls, and to become a nun therein. At other times I had thought of depositing it in the Bank of France, and purchasing an inalienable annuity for Leoni, which would keep him from want and villainy forever. I should have retained for myself only a modest annuity, and have buried myself alone in the Swiss valley where the memory of my happiness would assist me to endure the horror of solitude. When I learned the new disaster that had befallen Leoni, I felt that my love and anxiety for him sprang into life, more intense than ever. I sent all my fortune to a banking house at Milan. I reserved only a sufficient amount to double the pension which my father had bequeathed to my aunt. That amount was represented, to her great satisfaction, by the house in which we lived and in which she had passed half of her life. I abandoned it to her and set out to join Leoni. She did not ask me where I was going; she knew only too well; she did not try to detain me, she did not thank me, she simply pressed my hand; but when I turned to look back, I saw rolling slowly down her wrinkled cheek the first tear I had ever known her to shed.

21

XXII

I found Leoni in a horrible condition, haggard, pale as
death and almost mad. It was the first time that want
and suffering had really taken hold of him. Hitherto he
had simply seen his wealth vanish little by little, while
seeking and finding means to replenish it. His disasters
in that respect had been great; but card-sharping and
chance had never left him long battling with the privations of poverty. His mental power had always remained intact, but it was overcome when physical
strength abandoned him. I found him in a state of nervous
excitement which resembled madness. I gave securities
for his debt. It was easy for me to furnish proofs of my
responsibility, for I had them upon me. So I entered his
prison only to set him free. His joy was so intense that
he could not endure it, and he had to be carried, unconscious, to a carriage.

I took him to Florence and surrounded him with all the
comforts I could procure. When all his debts were paid,
I had very little left. I devoted all my energies to making him forget the sufferings of his prison. His robust
body was soon cured, but his mind remained diseased.
The terrors of darkness and the agony of despair had
made a profound impression upon that active, enterprising man, accustomed to the enioyments of wealth, or to
the excitement of the adventurer's life. Inaction had
shattered him. He had become subject to childish terrors, to terrible outbreaks of violence; he could not en-

dure the slightest annoyance; and the most horrible
thing was that he vented his wrath on me for all the
annoyances that I could not spare him. He had lost that
will power which enabled him to face without fear the
most precarious prospects for the future. He was terrified now at the thought of poverty and asked me every
day what resources I should have when my present
means were exhausted. I was appalled myself at the
thought of the destitution which was impending. The
time came at last. I began to paint pictures on screens,
snuff-boxes and other small articles of Spa wood. When
I had worked ten hours, my earnings amounted to eight
or ten francs. That would have been enough for my
needs; but for Leoni it was utter poverty. He longed
for a hundred impossible things; he complained bitterly,
savagely, because he was not richer. He often reproached me for having paid his debts and for not having fled with him and with my money too. To calm him,
I was obliged to convince him that it would have been
impossible for me to get him out of prison and commit that
piece of rascality. He would stand at the windows and
swear horribly at the rich people driving by in their carriages. He would point to his shabby clothes and say
with an accent that I cannot possibly imitate: *"Can't*
you help me to obtain a better coat? *Won't* you do it?"
He finally told me so often that I could rescue him from
his distress, and that it was cruel and selfish of me to
leave him in that condition, that I thought that he was
mad and no longer tried to argue with him on the subject.
I held my peace whenever he recurred to it, and concealed my tears, which served only to irritate him. He
thought that I understood his abominable hints and called
my silence inhuman indifference and stupid obstinacy.
Several times he struck me savagely and would have

killed me if some one had not come to my assistance. It
is true that when these paroxysms had passed, he threw
himself at my feet and implored me with tears in his eyes
to forgive him.   But I avoided these scenes of reconcilia-
tion so far as I could, for the emotion caused a fresh
shock to his nerves and provoked a return of the outbreaks.   At last this irritability ceased and gave place to
a sort of dull, stupid despair which was even more horrible.   He would gaze at me with a gloomy expression,
and seemed to nourish a secret aversion for me and
projects of revenge.   Sometimes I woke in the middle of
the night and saw him standing by my bed, his face
wearing a sinister expression; at such times I thought
that he meant to kill me, and I shrieked with fear.   But
he would simply shrug his shoulders and return to his
bed with a stupid laugh.

In spite of everything I loved him still, not as he was,
but because of what he had been and might become
again.   There were times when I had hopes that a
blessed revolution was taking place in him, and that he
would come forth from that crisis a new man, cleansed of
all his evil inclinations.   He seemed no longer to think of
satisfying them, nor did he express regret or desire for anything whatsoever.   I could not imagine the subject of the
long meditations by which he seemed to be absorbed.
Most of the time his eyes were fixed upon me with such a
strange expression that I was afraid of him.   I dared not
speak to him, but I asked his forgiveness by imploring
glances.   Then I would imagine that his own glance
melted and that his breast rose with an imperceptible
sigh; he would turn his head away as if he wished to
conceal or stifle his emotion, and would fall to musing
again.   At such times I flattered myself that he was en-
gaged in making salutary reflections concerning the past,

and that he would soon open his heart to tell me that he had conceived a hatred of vice and a love of virtue.

My hopes grew fainter when the Marquis de —— reappeared on the scene. He never entered my apartments, because he knew the horror I had of him; but he would pass under the windows and call Leoni, or come to my door and knock in a peculiar way to let him know that he was there. Then Leoni would go out with him and remain away a long while. One day I saw them pass and repass several times; the Vicomte de Chalm was with them.

"Leoni is lost," I thought, "and I too; some fresh crime will soon be committed under my eyes."

That evening Leoni came home late; and, as he left his companions at the street door, I heard him say these words:

"But you can tell her that I am mad, absolutely mad; and that otherwise I would never have consented to it. She must know well enough that want has driven me mad."

I dared not ask him for any explanation, and I served his modest supper. He did not touch it but began to poke the fire nervously; then he asked me for ether, and, having taken a large dose, went to bed and seemed to sleep. I worked every evening as long as I could, until I was overcome by drowsiness and fatigue. That night I went to bed at midnight. I was hardly in bed when I heard a slight noise, and it seemed to me that Leoni was dressing to go out. I spoke to him and asked what he was doing.

"Nothing," he said, "I was just getting up to come to you; but I don't like your light, you know that it affects my nerves and gives me horrible pains in the head; put it out."

I obeyed.

"Have you done it?" he said. "Now go to bed again, I am coming to kiss you; wait a moment."

This mark of affection, which he had not bestowed upon me for several weeks, made my poor heart leap with joy and hope. I flattered myself that the revival of his affection would lead to the recovery of reason and conscience. I sat on the edge of my bed and awaited him with the utmost joy. He came and threw himself into my arms, which were wide open to receive him, and, embracing me passionately, threw me back upon my bed. But, at that instant, a feeling of distrust, due to the protection of heaven or the delicacy of my instinct, led me to pass my hand over the face of the man who was embracing me. Leoni had allowed his beard and moustaches to grow since he had been ill; I found a smooth, clean-shaven face. I gave a shriek and pushed him away with all my force.

"What is the matter?" said Leoni's voice.

"Have you shaved your beard," I said.

"As you see," he replied.

But I noticed that while his voice was speaking at my ear, another mouth was clinging to mine. I shook myself free with the strength which wrath and despair give, and, rushing to the other end of the room, hurriedly turned up the lamp, which I had lowered but had not put out. I saw Lord Edwards seated on the edge of the bed, bewildered and disconcerted,—I believe that he was drunk,—and Leoni coming toward me with a desperate look in his eyes.

"Wretch!" I cried.

"Juliette," he said, with haggard eyes and in a muffled voice, "yield if you love me. It is a question of rescuing me from this destitution, in which, as you see, I am eating my heart out. It is a question of life and reason with me, as you know. My salvation will be the reward of your devotion ; and, as for yourself, you will be rich and happy with a man who has loved you for a long while, and who considers no price too great to pay to obtain you. Consent, Juliette," he added under his breath, "or I will kill you when he has left the room."

Terror deprived me of all judgment. I jumped through the window at the risk of killing myself. Some soldiers who were passing picked me up and carried me into the house unconscious. When I came to myself, Leoni and his confederates had left the house. They declared that I had jumped from the window in the delirium of brain fever, while they had gone into another room to call for help. They had feigned the greatest consternation. Leoni had remained until the surgeon who attended me declared that I had broken no bones. Then he had gone out saying that he would return, but he had not been seen for two days. He did not return, and I never saw him again.

Here Juliette finished her narrative and fell back on her couch, overwhelmed with fatigue and sadness.

"It was then, my poor child," I said, "that I made your acquaintance. I was living in the same house. The story of your accident aroused my interest. Soon I learned that you were young and worthy of a serious attachment ; that Leoni, after treating you with great brutality, had abandoned you when you were critically ill and in want. I desired to see you ; you were delirious when I approached your bed. O, Juliette, how lovely you were, with your bare shoulders, your dishevelled hair, your lips burning with the fire of fever, and your face animated by the excitement of suffering ! How lovely you still seemed to me when, prostrated by fa-

tigue, you fell back on your pillow, pale and drooping,
like a white rose shedding its leaves in the hot sun of
midday! I could not tear myself away from you. I felt
a thrill of irresistible sympathy; I was impelled by such
a deep interest as nobody had ever aroused in me. I
sent for the leading physicians of the city; I procured
for you all the comforts that you lacked. Poor deserted
girl! I passed whole nights by your bedside, I saw your
despair, I understood your love. I had never loved; it
seemed to me that no woman was capable of returning the
passion that I was capable of feeling. I sought a heart as
fervent as mine. I distrusted all those that I put to the test,
and I soon realized the prudence of my self-restraint when
I saw the coldness and frivolity of the hearts of those
women. Yours seemed to me the only one capable of understanding me. A woman who could love and suffer as
you had done was the realization of all my dreams. I desired to obtain your affection, but without much hope of
success. What gave me the presumption to try to console
you was my absolute certainty that I loved you sincerely
and generously. All that you said in your delirium
taught me to know you just as well and thoroughly as
our subsequent intimacy has done. I knew that you were
a sublime creature from the prayers that you addressed
to God, aloud, in a tone of which no words can describe
the heart-rending purity. You prayed for forgiveness
for Leoni, always forgiveness, never vengeance! You
invoked the souls of your parents; you described to
them breathlessly the misfortunes by which you had
expiated your flight and their sorrow. Sometimes you
took me for Leoni, and poured out crushing reproaches
upon me; at other times you thought that you were with
him in Switzerland, and you embraced me passionately.
It would have been easy for me then to abuse your error,

and the love that was gaining headway in my breast
made your frantic caresses a veritable torture. But I
would have died rather than yield to my desires, and the
villainy of Lord Edwards, of which you talked constantly,
seems to me the most degrading infamy of which a man
could be guilty. At last I had the good fortune to save
your life and your reason, my dear Juliette. Since then
I have suffered bitterly, and I have been very happy
through you. I am a fool perhaps not to be content
with the friendship and the possession of such a woman
as you, but my love is insatiable. I long to be loved as
Leoni was, and I torment you with that foolish ambition.
I have not his eloquence and his fascinations, but I love
you. I have not deceived you ; I will never deceive
you. It is time for your heart, so long shattered by
fatigue, to find rest while sleeping on mine. Juliette !
Juliette ! when will you love me as you are capable of
loving ? ''

"Now and forever," she replied. "You saved me,
you cured me, and you love me. I was mad, I see it
now, to love such a man. All this that I have told you
has brought before my eyes anew a multitude of vile
things. Now I feel nothing but horror for the past, and
I do not mean to recur to it again. You have done well
to let me tell it all to you. I am calm now, and I feel
that I can never again love his memory. You are my
friend ; you are my savior, my brother and my lover."

"Say your husband too, Juliette, I implore you ! "

"My husband, if you will," she said, embracing me
with a fondness which she had never manifested so
warmly, and which brought tears of joy and gratitude
to my eyes.

XXIII

I awoke the next day so happy that I thought no more about leaving Venice. The weather was superb, the sun as mild as in spring. Fashionably dressed women thronged the quays and laughed at the jests of the maskers, who, half reclining on the rails of the bridges, teased the passers-by, and made impertinent and flattering remarks to the ugly and pretty women respectively. It was Mardi Gras; a sad anniversary for Juliette. I was anxious to distract her thoughts, so suggested that we should go out, and she agreed.

I looked proudly at her as she walked by my side. It is not the custom to offer one's arm to a lady in Venice, but simply to support her by grasping her elbow as you go up and down the white marble stairways which confront you whenever you cross a canal. Juliette was so graceful and lithe in all her movements that I took a childish delight in feeling her lean gently on my hand as we crossed the bridges. Everybody turned to look at her, and the women, who never take pleasure in another woman's beauty, observed with interest, at all events, the refinement of her dress and her bearing, which they would have been glad to copy. It seems to me that I can still see Juliette's costume and her graceful figure. She wore a gown of violet velvet with an ermine boa and small muff. Her white satin hat framed her face, which was still pale, but so exquisitely beautiful that, despite seven or eight years of fatigue and mental unhappiness,

no one thought her more than eighteen. She wore violet
silk stockings, so transparent that one could see through
them the alabaster whiteness of her flesh. When she
had passed and her face could no longer be seen, people
followed with their eyes her tiny feet, so rare in Italy. I
was happy to have her thus admired; I told her so, and
she smiled at me with a sweet, affectionate expression.
God! how happy I was!

A gayly-decorated boat, filled with maskers and musicians, was coming along the Giudecca canal. I suggested
to Juliette that we take a gondola and row near to it, to
see the costumes. She assented. Several parties followed our example, and we soon found ourselves entan-
gled in a group of gondolas and skiffs which, with ourselves, accompanied the decorated vessel and seemed to
serve as an escort to it.

We heard the gondoliers say that the party of maskers
was composed of the richest and most fashionable young
men in Venice. They were, in truth, dressed with extreme magnificence; their costumes were very rich, and
the boat was decorated with silken sails, streamers of
silver gauze and Oriental rugs of very great beauty.
They were dressed like the ancient Venetians whom Paul
Veronese, by a happy anachronism, has introduced in
several devotional pictures, notably in the magnificent
Nuptials, which the Republic of Venice presented to
Louis XIV., and which is now in the Musée at Paris. I
noticed especially one man near the rail of the boat,
dressed in a long robe of pale green silk, embroidered
with long arabesques in gold and silver. He was standing,
and playing on the guitar; his attitude was so noble, his
tall figure so perfectly formed, that he seemed to have
been made expressly to wear those rich garments. I
called Juliette's attention to him; she looked up at him

mechanically, hardly seeing him, and answered: "Yes, yes, superb!" thinking of something else.

We continued to follow, and, being crowded by the other boats, touched the decorated vessel just where this man stood. Juliette was standing by my side and leaning against the awning of the gondola to avoid being thrown backward by the shocks we often received. Suddenly this man leaned toward Juliette as if to see her more distinctly, passed his guitar to his neighbor, tore off his black mask and turned toward us again. I saw his face, which was beautiful and noble, if ever human face was. Juliette did not see him. Thereupon he called her name in an undertone, and she started as if she had received an electric shock.

"Juliette!" he repeated in a louder voice.

"Leoni!" she cried, frantic with joy.

It is still like a dream to me. A mist passed before my eyes; I lost the sense of sight for a second, I believe. Juliette rushed forward, impulsively and with energy. Suddenly I saw her transported as if by magic to the other boat, into Leoni's arms; their lips met in a delirious kiss. The blood rushed to my brain, roared in my ears, covered my eyes with a thicker veil. I do not know what happened. I came to myself as I was entering the hotel. I was alone; Juliette had gone with Leoni.

I flew into a frenzy of passion, and for three hours I raved like an epileptic. Toward night I received a letter from Juliette, thus conceived:

"Forgive me, forgive me, Bustamente; I love you, I respect you and I bless you on my knees for your love and your benefactions. Do not hate me; you know that I do not belong to myself, that an invisible hand controls my actions and throws me against my will into that man's

arms. O my friend, forgive me and do not seek revenge.
I love him, I cannot live without him. I cannot know
that he exists without longing for him, I cannot see him
pass without following him. I am his wife, you see, and
he is my master; it is impossible for me to escape from
his passion and his authority. You saw whether I was
able to resist his summons. There was something like
an electric current, a magnet, which lifted me up and drew
me to his heart, and yet I was by your side, I had my
hand in yours. Why did you not hold me back? you
had not the power; your hand opened, your lips were
powerless to call me back; you see that it is beyond our
control. There is a hidden will, a magic power, which
ordains and accomplishes these strange things. I cannot
break the chain that binds me to Leoni, it is the fetter
that couples galley-slaves, but it was God's hand that
welded it.

"O my dear Aleo, do not curse me! I am at your
feet. I implore you to let me be happy. If you knew
how dearly he loves me still, with what joy he received
me! what caresses, what words, what tears! I am
as one drunk, I seem to be dreaming. I must forget
his crime against me: he was mad. After deserting me,
he reached Naples in such a state of mental alienation
that he was confined in an insane asylum. I do not know
by what miracle he was cured and discharged, nor to
what lucky chance he owes it that he is now once more
at the very pinnacle of wealth. But he is handsomer,
more brilliant, more passionate than ever. Let me, oh!
let me love him, though I am destined to be happy but a
single day and to die to-morrow. Should not you forgive
me for loving him so madly, you who have an equally
blind and misplaced passion for me?

"Forgive me; I am mad; I know not what I am saying nor what it is that I ask you. It is not to take me back and forgive me when he has abandoned me again; oh, no! I have too much pride, never fear. I feel that I no longer deserve you, that when I rushed into that boat I cut myself adrift from you forever, that I can never again look you in the face or touch your hand. Adieu then, Aleo! Yes, I am writing to bid you adieu, for I cannot part from you without telling you that my heart is already bleeding, and that it will break some day with regret and repentance. I tell you, you will be avenged! Calm yourself now, forgive, pity me, pray for me; be sure that I am no insensible ingrate who does not appreciate your character and her duty to you. I am only an unhappy creature whom fatality drives hither and thither, and who has not the power to stop. I turn my face to you and send you a thousand farewells, a thousand kisses, a thousand blessings. But the tempest envelopes me and carries me off. As I perish on the reefs on which it is certain to hurl me, I will repeat your name and invoke your intercession as an angel of forgiveness between God and me.

"JULIETTE."

This letter caused a fresh attack of frenzy; then I fell into despair; I sobbed like a child for several hours; and, succumbing to fatigue, I fell asleep in my chair, in that vast room where Juliette had told me her story the night before. I awoke more calm; I lighted the fire and paced the floor back and forth several times with slow and measured step.

As the day was breaking I fell asleep again: my mind was made up; I was calm. At nine o'clock I went and made inquiries throughout the city, trying to get information as to certain details which I needed to know about. Nobody knew by what means Leoni had made his fortune ; it was known simply that he was rich, extravagant and dissipated ; all the men of fashion frequented his house, copied his dress and were his companions in debauchery. The Marquis de —— accompanied him everywhere and shared his opulence ; both were in love with a famous courtesan, and, by virtue of a most extraordinary caprice, that woman refused their offers. Her resistance had so stimulated Leoni's desire that he had made her the most extravagant promises, and there was no folly into which she could not lead him.

I called at her house and had much trouble in obtaining an audience. I was admitted at last, and she received me with a haughty air, asking me what I wanted, in the tone of a person who is in a hurry to dismiss an importunate caller.

"I have come to ask a favor at your hands," I said.

"You hate Leoni ? "

"Yes, I hate him mortally."

"May I ask you why ? "

"He seduced a young sister of mine at Friuli, a virtuous, saint-like child ; she died in the hospital. I would like to eat Leoni's heart."

"Meanwhile, will you assist me to play a cruel practical joke on him ? "

"Yes."

"Will you write to him and give him an assignation ? "

"Yes, provided that I do not keep it."

"That is understood. Here is a sketch of the note you must write him :

"I know that you have found your wife again and that you love her. I did not want you yesterday, you seemed too easy a conquest; to-day it seems to me that it will be interesting to make you unfaithful; moreover, I am anxious to know if your frantic desire to possess me makes you capable of everything, as you boast. I know that you are to give a concert on the water this evening; I will be in a gondola and will follow you. You know my gondolier, Cristofano; be near the rail of your boat and leap into my gondola as soon as you see it. I will keep you an hour, after which I shall have had enough of you forever, perhaps. I want none of your presents; I want only this proof of your love. This evening or never."

La Misana thought the note very singular in tone and copied it laughingly.

"What will you do with him when you have him in the gondola ? "

"Set him ashore on the bank of the Lido and let him pass a long, cool night there."

"I would gladly kiss you to show my gratitude," said the courtesan; "but I have a lover whom I propose to love all the week. Adieu."

"You must place your gondolier at my orders," I said.

"To be sure; he is intelligent, discreet and strong; do with him as you will."

XXIV

I returned to the hotel and passed the rest of the day reflecting deeply upon what I was to do. Night came; Cristofano and the gondola were waiting under my window. I dressed myself like a gondolier; Leoni's boat appeared, decorated with colored lanterns, which gleamed like gems, from the top of the masts to the end of every piece of rigging, and sending up rockets in all directions in the intervals between the bursts of music. I stood at the stern of the gondola, oar in hand; I rowed alongside. Leoni was by the rail, in the same costume as on the night before; Juliette was sitting among the musicians; she too wore a magnificent costume, but she was downcast and pensive, and seemed not to be thinking of him. Cristofano removed his hat and raised his lantern to the level of his face. Leoni recognized him and leaped into the gondola.

As soon as he was on board, Cristofano informed him that La Misana was awaiting him in another gondola near the public garden.

"What's that? why isn't she here?" he asked.

"*Non so,*" replied the gondolier indifferently, and he began to row. I seconded him vigorously, and in a few moments we had passed the public garden. We were surrounded by a dense mist. Leoni leaned forward several times and asked if we were not almost there. We continued to glide smoothly over the placid surface of the lagoon; the moon, pale and swathed in mist, whitened the atmosphere without lightening it. We passed like smugglers the line which cannot ordinarily be passed without a permit from the police, and did not pause until we reached the sandy bank of the Lido, far enough away to be in no danger of meeting a living being.

"Knaves!" cried our prisoner. "Where the devil have you taken me? Where are the stairways of the public gardens? Where is La Misana's gondola? *Ventre-Dieu!* We are on sand! You have gone astray in the mist, clowns that you are, and you have set me ashore at random——"

22

"No, signor," I said in Italian; "be kind enough to take ten steps with me and you will find the person you seek."

He followed me; whereupon Cristofano, in accordance with my orders, instantly rowed away with the gondola, and went to wait for me in the lagoon on the other side of the island.

"Will you stop, brigand?" cried Leoni, when we had walked along the beach for several minutes. "Do you wish me to freeze here? Where is your mistress? Where are you taking me?"

"Signor," I rejoined, turning and drawing from under my cape the objects I had brought, "allow me to light your path."

With that I produced my dark lantern, opened it, and hung it on one of the posts on the bank.

"What the devil are you doing there?" he said; "have I a madman to deal with? What does this mean?"

"It means," I said, taking the swords from beneath my cloak, "that you must fight with me."

"With you, you cur! I'll beat you as you deserve."

"One moment," I said, taking him by the collar with an energy which staggered him a little. "I am not what you think; I am noble as well as yourself. Moreover, I am an honest man and you are a scoundrel. Therefore I do you much honor by fighting with you."

It seemed to me that my adversary trembled and was inclined to run away. I pressed him more closely.

"What do you want of me?" he cried. "Damnation! who are you? I don't know you. Why have you brought me here? Do you mean to murder me? I have no money about me. Are you a thief?"

"No," I said, "there is no thief and murderer here but yourself, as you well know."

"Are you my enemy?"

"Yes, I am your enemy."

"What is your name?"

"That does not concern you ; you will find out if you kill me."

"And what if I don't choose to kill you?" he cried, shrugging his shoulders and struggling to appear self-possessed.

"In that case you will allow me to kill you," I replied, "for I give you my word that one of us two is destined to remain here to-night."

"You are a villain," he cried, making frantic efforts to escape. "Help! help!"

"That is quite useless," I said; "the noise of the waves drowns your voice, and you are a long way from human help. Keep quiet, or I will strangle you. Don't lose your temper, but make the most of the chances of safety I give you. I propose to kill you, not murder you. You know what that means. Fight with me, and do not compel me to take advantage of my superior strength, which must be evident to you."

As I spoke, I shook him by the shoulders and made him bend like a reed, although he was a full head taller than I. He realized that he was at my mercy, and tried to argue with me.

"But, signor," he said, "if you are not mad, you must have some reason for fighting with me. What have I done to you?"

"It does not please me to tell you," I replied, "and you are a coward to ask for my reasons for revenge, when you should demand satisfaction of me."

"What for?" he rejoined. "I never saw you before. It is not light enough for me to distinguish your features, but I am sure that this is the first time that I ever heard your voice."

"Dastard, have you no cause to be revenged on a man who has made sport of you, who has procured an assignation to be given you in order to play a joke upon you, and who has brought you here against your will to insult you? I was told that you were brave. Must I strike you to arouse your courage?"

"You are an insolent scoundrel," he said, making an effort to work himself into a passion.

"Very good! I demand satisfaction for that remark, and I propose to take satisfaction at once with this blow."

I struck him lightly on the cheek. He uttered a roar of rage and fear.

"Have no fear," I said, holding him with one hand and giving him a sword with the other. "Defend yourself. I know that you are the first swordsman in Europe; I am far from being your equal. It is true that I am calm and you are frightened, which equalizes our chances."

Giving him no time to reply, I attacked him fiercely. The wretch threw his sword away and ran. I followed him, overtook him and shook him furiously. I threatened to throw him into the sea and drown him if he did not defend himself. When he saw that it was impossible for him to escape, he took the sword and mustered that desperate courage which love of life and unavoidable danger give to the most timid. But whether because the feeble light of the lantern did not allow him to measure his blows accurately, or because the fright he had experienced had taken away all his presence of mind, I found this terrible duellist pitifully weak. I was so determined not to slaughter him that I spared him a long while. At last he threw himself upon my sword, when trying to feint, and spitted himself up to the hilt.

"Justice! justice!" he said as he fell. "I am murdered!"

"You demand justice and you obtain it," I replied.
"You die by my hand as Henryet died by yours."

He uttered a dull roar, bit the sand and gave up the
ghost.

I took the two swords and started to find the gondola;
but as I crossed the island I was seized with a thousand
unfamiliar emotions. My strength suddenly failed me;
I sat down upon one of those Hebraic tombs, half
covered by the grass, which are ceaselessly beaten by
the sharp salt winds from the Adriatic. The morn was
beginning to come forth from the mist, and the white
stones of that vast cemetery stood out against the dark
verdure of the Lido. I reflected upon what I had done,
and my revenge, from which I had anticipated so much
joy, appeared to me in a most distressing light; I felt
something like remorse, and yet I had thought that it was
a legitimate and blessed act to purge the earth of that
fiend incarnate and deliver Juliette from him. But I had
not expected to find him a coward. I had hoped to meet
a bold swordsman, and in attacking him I had thought
that I was sacrificing my life. I was disturbed and almost appalled to have taken his life so easily. I did not
find that my hatred was satisfied by vengeance, but I
did feel that it was extinguished by contempt.—"When
I found what a coward he was," I thought, "I should
have spared him; I should have forgotten my resentment
against him and my love for a woman capable of prefer-
ring such a man to me."

Thereupon confused, painful, agitated thoughts rushed
into my brain. The cold, the darkness, the sight of
those tombs calmed me at intervals; they plunged me
into a dreamy stupor from which I awoke with a violent
and painful shock when I suddenly remembered my situation, Juliette's despair, which would burst forth on the

morrow, and the aspect of that corpse lying on the blood-
stained sand not far away.

"Perhaps he is not dead," I thought.

I had a vague desire to go to see. I would almost
have been glad to restore him to life. The first rays of
dawn surprised me in this irresolute frame of mind, and
I reflected that prudence required me to leave that spot.
I went and found Cristofano, who was sound asleep in
his gondola, and whom I had much difficulty in waking.
The sight of that placid slumber aroused my envy. Like
Macbeth, I had taken leave of it for a long time to come.

I returned, gently rocked by the waves which the
approach of the sun had already tipped with pink. I
passed quite near the steamboat which runs from Venice
to Trieste. It was its hour for starting; the wheels were
already beating the water into foam, and red sparks flew
upward from the funnel, with columns of black smoke.
Several boats brought belated passengers. A gondola
grated against ours and made fast to the packet. A man
and woman left that gondola and ran lightly up the
gangway. They were no sooner on the deck than the
steamer started at full speed. The couple leaned over
the rail to watch the wake. I recognized Juliette and
Leoni. I thought that I was dreaming; I passed my
hand over my eyes and called to Cristofano:

"Is that Baron Leone de Leoni starting for Trieste
with a lady?"

"Yes, signor," he replied.

I uttered a horrible oath; then recalling the gondolier,
I asked him:

"Who in God's name was the man we took to the
Lido last night?"

"Why, as your Excellency knows," he replied, "it
was Marquis Lorenzo de ——."